S0-BDL-275

byte

byte

a novel

Eric C. Anderson

db
dunn books

Published by Dunn Books
First edition November 2018
This title is also available as a Dunn Books ebook.

This book is a work of fiction. Any references to historical events, real people, or real places are used fictitiously. Other names, characters, places, and events are products of the author's imagination. Any resemblance to actual events, places, or people—living or dead—is pure coincidence.

Library of Congress cataloging-in-publication data is on file with the U.S. Copyright Office.

Hardcover ISBN: 978-0-9985742-1-9
Paperback ISBN: 978-0-9985742-0-2
Ebook ISBN: 978-0-9985742-2-6

Designed by Archie Ferguson
Maps by Joe LeMonnier

Manufactured in the United States of America

For Sven, he planted the idea...
I'll take the blame for what follows

The internet is the first thing that humanity has
built that humanity doesn't understand,
the largest experiment in anarchy we ever had.

—Eric Schmidt, Google CEO

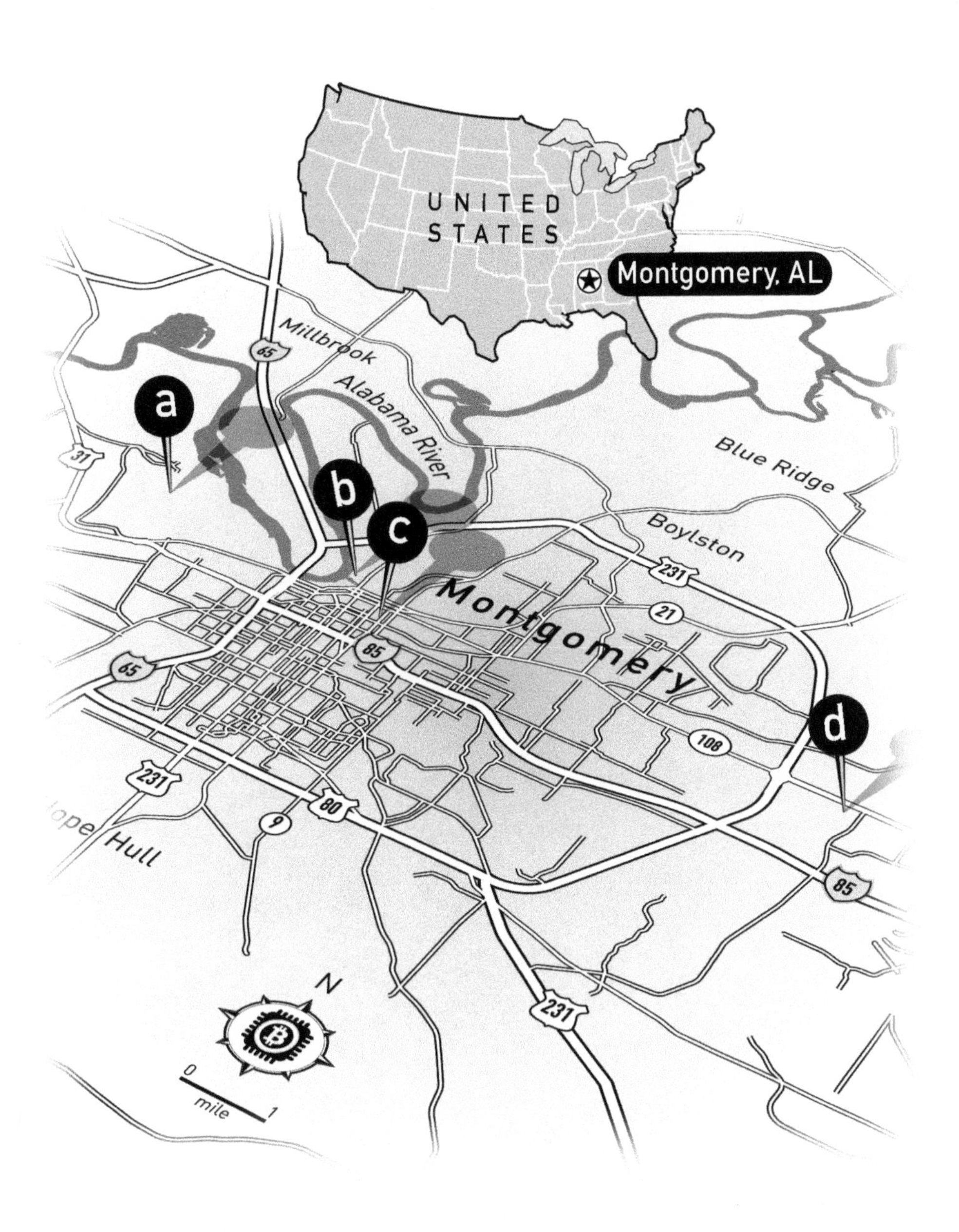

a Maxwell AF Base
b Biscuits Riverwalk Stadium
b Renaissance Hotel
c State Capitol
d Mr Gus' Ristorante

- a Ostankino Tower
- b Patriarch's Ponds
- c Smolenskaya Metro
- c Bulat Oskavjava Monument
- c White Rabbit
- d New Arbat Ave.
- e Red Square, The Kremlin
- f Gorky Park

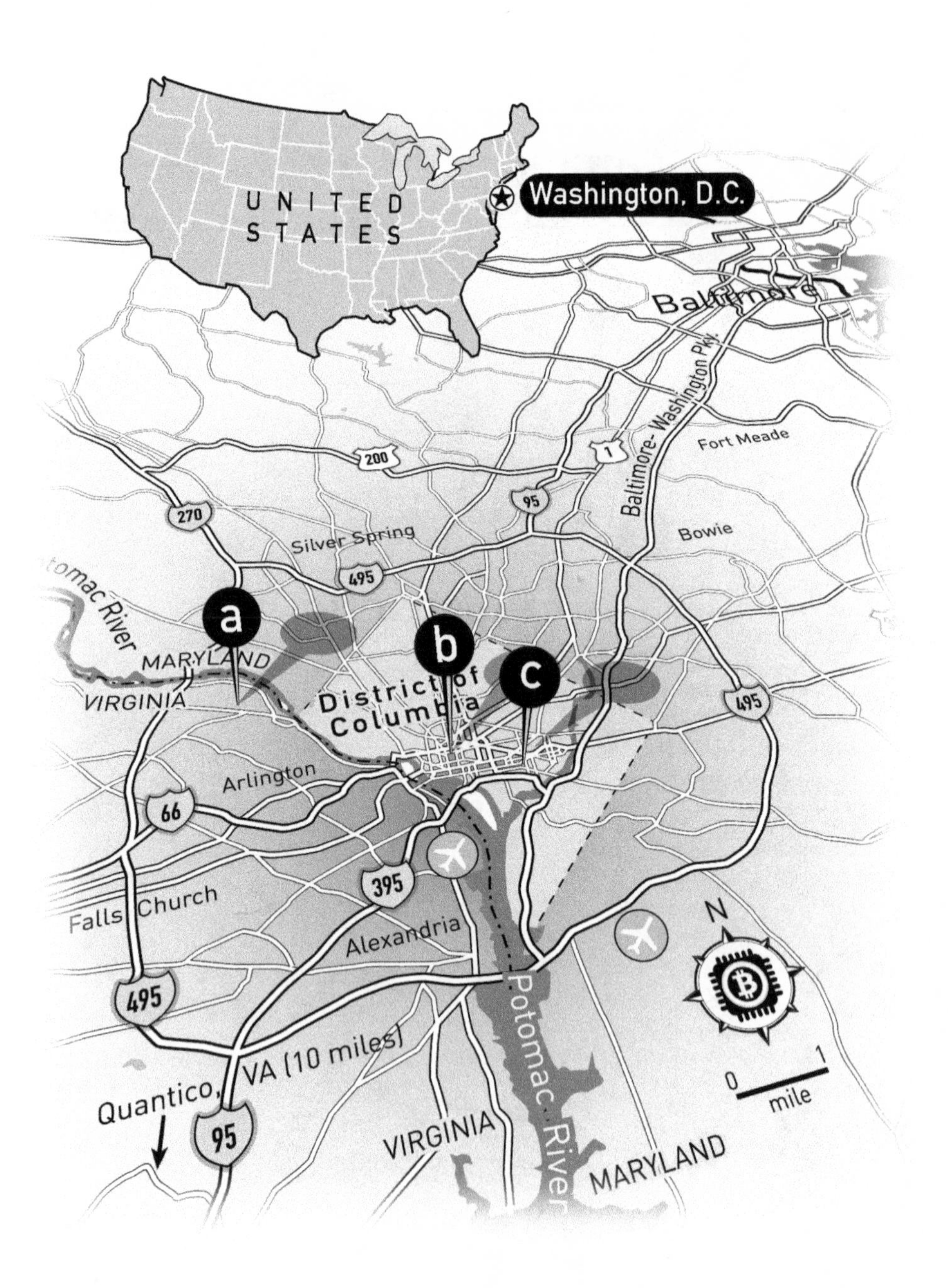

a CIA HQ in Langley, VA
b The White House
c Capitol Hill
c Eastern Market

byte

To understand what constitutes a *byte* one must know about *bits.*

A *bit,* shorthand for a "binary digit," is the fundamental element of computer coding. A *bit* has but two values . . . zero or one. In essence, "yes" or "no." Something is on or off, or is not resident. This perhaps helps explain why developing artificial intelligence is so difficult. Your computer does not "think" in shades of gray. A statement is either "true" or it is "false," no room for negotiation.

A *byte* was normally composed of eight *bits.* Mathematically, in the event you are curious, this made possible 0 to 255 different combinations—a traditional keyboard had only 101 keys. Life was good. At eight *bits* early programmers could encode a single character of text. Like "1" or the letter "A." This makes a *byte* the most diminutive element of coding that computers entertain when processing a command. Yes, the *bit* is still present, but to speed things up—well, the machine hunts *bytes.*

As we pushed technology forward the *byte* got bigger. Today it is not unusual to encounter forty-eight *bits* in a *byte.* Blame it on our fascination with object-oriented navigation. Seems humans like pictures rather than words. That's why finding a DOS prompt on your laptop requires a lot of finagling. DOS worked in eight-*bit* collections of *bytes.* That cell phone you randomly toss on the kitchen counter ain't that simple.

b y t e

prologue

blue screen of death

I came to in a sterile white room. Collection of nervous faces staring down. A variety of beeps and tones suggested there was a sea of medical gear monitoring vital signs somewhere behind my head. Would have turned to check out the screens, but my cranium was pinned in place. Some goddamn strap across my forehead. Couldn't move my arms either. Seems they were tied to the bedrails. Looking down I could just catch sight of the leather bands around each wrist.

Shit, did I go nuts and try to kill a crowd of schoolchildren?

To be honest, I don't exactly remember the last moments of ambulatory life. That is, the seconds before my legs ceased being useful for transportation. Before the wheelchair. I like to refer to that time period as "BC," Before Chair. The remainder is "AC," After Chair.

Momma was there. One of the crowd. Looking worried.

"Honey, can you hear me?"

Stupid question. Of course I could hear her, just couldn't move.

"You've had an accident."

That was all it took to reignite memories.

I always loved that red Ducati ST4S. Fucking Italians know how to build a bike. I owned a 2005, came with a 996cc twin-cylinder engine. Put out 120 horses, I'd seen 151 miles an hour on a track—*after* you pulled off the two hard case pillions (that would be saddlebags for those of you who don't speak motorcycle). Rode that damn thing everywhere. Once went by a cop on the Washington, DC, beltway at a little over 130 mph, he didn't even turn on his lights. Wasn't going to catch me on that machine.

Sitting in front of a computer for a living makes for a fat ass and boredom. So, I found every racetrack in the area and spent my weekends racing against kids with the new 600 or 750cc street bikes. My daddy used to say, "There's no replacement for displacement." He was right. The punks would scoff, "Hey babe, you gonna hafta scrap that antique after I school you."

Nothing better than going past one of those assholes with the front end off the ground. Sometimes, if they were real morons, I'd flash them the bird before setting that spinning front wheel back down on the tarmac. Never fuck with an angry black woman. And I was a *very* angry black woman on a track with that Ducati between my legs.

Damn, I miss that bike.

One of the punks with a 750cc "naked" street machine slammed me into a track wall after *he* lost control. Must've been doing about 120 when I hit the concrete. An expensive helmet will save your head; it does nothing for your spine or limbs. Would've been nice if the punk died. Me, I hit the fucking wall and my world went dark.

Turned out it stayed dark for about two weeks. Or so Momma said. What did I know, I hadn't been present for the last fourteen or so days.

Eventually learned I'd been airlifted to the Virginia Hospital Center. Reset the broken left leg, put pins in my crushed right hand, and ran a set of plates with screws into the left upper arm to get that straight. In other words, I broke a lot of shit. Including a spinal compression that put an end to my days of heading to the bars for hours of dancing with the latest hot date. Now I was AC. After Chair.

About that helmet. Owned an Arai Signet-Q. A thousand-dollar gift to myself. Figured if you work over a keyboard it was a good idea to protect the shit between your ears. Still have the helmet. It's scarred and the visor is gone. Think the medical crews pulled it off to facilitate resuscitation. Shit, I wasn't dead, just broken. Should've left me the visor.

These days the helmet sits on a shelf above my work desk, next to the trophies and pictures of past glories.

Only black woman to win the amateur track title three years in a row. Man, my face appeared in pictures on pages of the fucking *Washington Post.* Try pulling that off when you're a thirty-five-year-old computer programmer riding a fifteen-year-old motorcycle against kids with mommies and daddies happy to purchase them the latest fast toy.

Being handicapped doesn't make you stupid. Went home after four weeks. Worst food you ever ate. Made Momma bring my computer from home so I could work... or at least check emails.

She didn't go into my house very often, was appalled at the cleanliness, or lack thereof. Who has time to clean and dust when it's the height of racing season? I bet the guys all lived in slightly less than white-glove conditions as well.

That's not being fair to myself. The office and accompanying machines were meticulous. I could never work in the midst of a disaster. Everything has a place in this office, and it goes back there at the end of every day, regardless of what time I finish. Don't pay too much attention to the clock, just know that every morning starts with a trip to the gym and every evening ends with two shots of straight-up Jack Daniel's. Puts the brain on hold for the four to six hours I use to recharge my batteries before starting another round at the damn keyboard.

Seems boring, doesn't it? Sit in the house all day and combat the *bits* and *bytes.* Would be boring if I didn't have that Tesla Model X for transportation (540 ponies... faster than the damn Ducati from 0 to 60) and a job that allowed me to play in everyone's—*everyone's*—backyard.

Might want to think about what you have on that home computer the next time junior decides to go surf the web. Chances are, I have a copy of your files on one of the storage devices mounted in a rack parked in a former walk-in closet just to the left of my desk.

My employer, a certain government agency, wasn't happy about losing me for four weeks of medical downtime. But they sure as hell weren't gonna lay me off. Didn't care if I demanded my work almost all be done from home. Never went into the office back when I was BC—Before Chair. Got it now?

What do I do? Let's put it this way—everyone has a secret, a vulnerability, and almost everyone makes a mistake when it comes time to secure those secrets and vulnerabilities. Particularly when you're talking about the digital world. Hide what you want, if you log that machine into the World Wide Web, well—*I will get in*. Fucking wheelchair ain't no impediment to cyber travel.

Oh, I'm not stupid. Think I said that before. People, a few anyway, figure out how to trace back where their data has gone astray. Keep a 9mm Beretta in a desk drawer, another in the bedroom, and a third tucked in a slot just beneath the wheelchair seat. Just need to remember to leave that in the car when I go to the office or airport. Don't feel like being strip-searched by some horny TSA idiot just 'cause the "cripple" came through security armed.

Anyway, they like me at the range. I can shoot with some of the best. At least if it's a target within twenty meters. Never enjoyed a "long gun," leave the elephant hunting for knuckle-dragging rich white guys.

Momma doesn't like the guns, but she has some idea of what I do…and knows I live alone. Hard to find a man who wants to date a sister confined to a wheelchair. Fuck them. If I want sex, well, women ain't the only prostitutes available online.

Welcome to my world.

Angry, middle-aged black woman riding about in a chair.

Just don't judge the book by its cover. I'm not bored. No blue screen of death on display here.

chapter 1

opening the kimono

washington, dc, 15 august 2025

Time for a little history lesson before I disappear into cyberspace.

I blame it all on Markus Hess. For the paltry sum of $54,000, this German citizen and his two counterparts managed to hack into academic, industrial, and military networks in Asia, Europe, and the United States.

And then sold the purloined data to the KGB—Moscow's premier intelligence agency back in the days when we still called Russia the Soviet Union.

I'm talking ancient history, 1985, 1986. Long before most of you were born and the internet was a public event.

Hess and company targeted ARPANET (Advanced Research Projects Agency Network) and MILNET (Military Network).

Without burying you in details, think of it this way: Uncle Sam wanted a means of linking computers back in the days when sneakers were the only means of transferring data. In other words, you had to put a floppy disk in a machine, download the data, remove the disk, and then get off your ass and walk to a colleague's office and hand them the floppy. He or she had to plug said floppy into their machine and load it. Depending on your file size—or number of files—this could take fifteen minutes or half a day.

Got worse if the coworker lived in another location. Then all your work got stuffed in an envelope and put through the snail mail system. Old white guys with trucks that had steering wheels on the wrong side and carried leather pouches stuffed with other people's crap. Meant there were a lot of ways for that data to get lost. Bad shit.

So, Uncle Sam came up with this ARPANET thing back in 1969. Rumor was that it was intended to survive a nuclear attack (or direct a nuclear attack, I can't recall the exact intent)—suffice it to say, it wasn't peaceful. Link the computers together via phone lines and then let users transfer communications—at a *real* slow pace. No pictures, no video, just words. But it eliminated the snail mail disaster and besides, no one did PowerPoint or online porn back in those days. ARPANET went live in 1970.

Fourteen years later it gave birth to MILNET.

Seems the boys in uniform weren't as dumb as some people like to claim. They linked up military headquarters and even the five-sided insane asylum, aka the Pentagon, via their piggyback onto ARPANET.

Life was so good, the academics decided they would have their own system of trading snarky observations and useless trivia. Called it BITNET (Because It's Time Network) and started linking universities together in 1981. I told you this stuff is ancient history.

Back to my story. Seems Hess and his accomplices discovered ARPANET and then discovered how easy it was to hack into the network. Back then if there was a password it was "administrator" or "password." A lot of places there was no password. Once you were in, you were *in.*

Lord knows how long those German kids got away with stealing data. Managed to break into machines associated with the U.S. Air Force, Army, and Navy. Wandered through files at the Jet Propulsion Laboratory in Pasadena and toured other, what we would now call "sensitive," locations. Passed all that good shit about aircraft technologies, satellites, semiconductors, and space on to our friends in Moscow.

Would have got away with it forever, at least in computer years.

Except Hess fucked up.

Incurred a seventy-five-cent, yes, a seventy-five-penny, charge, on a system at Lawrence Berkeley Laboratory. A charge that ignited the curiosity of a legend in the computer world—the now departed Clifford Stoll.

Stoll hunted down—in a manner that still amazes me—the world's first large-scale hackers. Even went to testify at Hess's trial in 1990. Like I said, the stuff of legends.

Before Hess and company, the worst threat was "phone phreakers," geeks who figured out how to bypass telephone bills via purloined digits or even humming at the right tone. That crap was amateur hour in comparison to what Hess had demonstrated. You could steal intellectual property from other people's computers—so long as they were hooked to a network—and then sell it to an interested party.

In this case, the KGB.

Funny, time passes, but the purchasing parties seem to remain the same. Just ask Hillary Clinton or the kids working at Microsoft, HP, and Amazon. Markets became so lucrative that Kaspersky Lab, a so-called internet security provider for all these devices we depend upon, wrote a backdoor into their code that down-loaded information to a mainframe at the Foreign Intelligence Service of the Russian Federation (SVR). Rumor has it SVR hands the best stuff right to the Kremlin—I presume that would be President Putin. But, who knows? Might be other interested consumers. And I'd bet there's more than one large corporation willing to pay for materials that provide a leg up on a competitor. It's a dog-eat-dog world, baby.

Problem we have here is that the story became focused on "stealing shit." Once Americans and the rest of the world were provided access to this internet thing back in 1991 there was seemingly no end to what a determined hacker could acquire. Want five million social security numbers and associated credit cards? We can do that. Need to "borrow" designs for the next silicon chip? We can do that. Want to read your political opponent's email? We can do that.

Left me working in a realm of petty thieves and pimple-faced teenagers. All of whom had seen *War Games*, that 1983 shlock about a teenager who almost starts World War III by hacking into a Pentagon computer, but seemingly lacked the imagination to do anything more interesting than downloading other people's stuff.

Yawn.

That ended in 2012 . . . yes, yes, still on ancient history. I wouldn't bore you with this crap, except what follows makes little sense without a bit of our past. And, baby, it is *our* past. You log onto a machine these days and this crap matters. Why do you think that annual bill for Norton is considered mandatory? Because what happens next changed the way we thought about the internet.

Yeah, that "benign" thing that you accept as a "necessity" has proven to be a real pain in the ass.

Now we go back in time . . . to 1988.

Meet my mentor, Robert Tappan Morris, now a professor emeritus at the Massachusetts Institute of Technology. Robert is a cool guy, even at age sixty. Unleashed the first "computer worm" in 1988 and was the first to be prosecuted under the U.S. Computer Fraud and Abuse Act back in 1990. And still managed to win tenure at MIT.

Talk about street cred. What Robert unleashed turned out to be the world's first denial of service application. Seems his attempt to discern the size of the budding internet flooded certain servers with requests for a response. Overwhelmed networks. Unintentional, but even then expensive—at least for the shuttered systems.

This became a favorite ploy for Russian hackers in the first decade of the twenty-first century.

Now we climb into the "I Love You" fiasco. May 2005. A pair of Filipino college idiots figured out how to write ten lines of code that exploited a flaw in Microsoft Outlook email software. Lonely users (apparently there are a lot of you out there) opened the attachment and caused more than 45 million computers worldwide to shut down.

I'm not sure who was dumber, the kids who wrote the code—they sure as shit made no money off the ploy—or the idiots who clicked on the attachment.

Fast forward to 2007. One of my favorites: "Poison Ivy." Nothing like taking advantage of expanding technologies. Put a camera on your computer, go online, and someone figures out how to turn on that eye in your machine without you knowing—I still use it today, twenty years after the original code hit the internet. You have no idea how many people keep a computer in their bedroom or positioned in an office where they jot notes on an easily observable white board. Get to watch everything in live action—there are bedrooms where the camera should be shut off to spare the viewer stomach unrest.

Still with me? This is the important crap. I'll spare you the multiple minor events.

We are now at April 2007. The Estonian government—long a victim of Russian colonialism—decided it was time to tear down a certain memorial to Soviet conquest. Seems Moscow didn't like the idea, so the Estonian banking service, highly dependent on the internet, suddenly was deluged with denial of service attacks. So much for using an ATM. Kids in the academic world declared this the first "cyber conflict."

Damn sure wouldn't be the last.

The Russians did it again in August 2008, when those pesky Georgians decided to break away from mother Moscow. Didn't shut down the systems—got fancy and replaced the home pages on government websites with anti-independence graffiti.

Turns out the Russians were rank fucking amateurs.

Ever hear of Stuxnet?

Ahhh, now *that's* some serious shit.

Back in 1998, the kids at NSA eventually discovered this thing called the internet and realized it might be a good idea to pay attention—as only NSA can. Stood up an organization called Tailored Access Operations or TAO (go look up "Taoism"—in China, Tao refers to an understanding of the underlying natural order of the Universe—modest bastards up there at Fort Meade).

On paper, the assigned personnel, largely a crew of twenty-somethings clad in dingy T-shirts and sneakers, were supposed to be breaking into adversary email and various digital exchanges.

In reality, they were a little more proactive.

They wrote some code that caused equipment in Iran's nascent nuclear program to spin off the rails. Called it Stuxnet. Cyber war went from denial and propaganda to physically destructive.

Cool.

About the same time Stuxnet was set loose, Washington established Cyber Command—aka CYBERCOM—and lashed it to NSA's hip. Now, you and I both know where this is going. Call something a "command" in the U.S. military system and suddenly there are people who want to exercise offensive capabilities. There's a reason North Korea built nukes—*we* have Pacific Command and Strategic Command. Bad karma if you're living in Pyongyang. Just ask Saddam Hussein—*he* fell victim to Central Command. Or Muammar Gaddafi—*he* caught the attention of Africa Command.

Get where I'm headed?

What Hess unleashed in 1985 has gone from just stealing shit to literally breaking things... or more appropriately, telling things to break themselves.

And we ain't alone. No, baby, it gets worse.

Keep marching up that timeline of hate and discontent in the world of bits and bytes. We're at August 2012. Employees at Saudi Aramco—Riyadh's oil monopoly—suddenly noticed their computers were not only malfunctioning, they were actually losing data right before the user's eyes. Best we could tell, Iran was sick of Saudi Arabian dominance in the Persian Gulf. Decided to teach the wealthy princes a lesson—corrupted more than thirty thousand computers. The only fix was replacement. Some smartass called it the Shamoon virus. (Looked it up once, Shamoon is a name implying you are meticulous, patient, and systematic—all too appropriate in this case; a second round of attacks visited Saudi computer systems in 2016 with equally devastating effects.)

The internet ain't funny no more, but is sure is a lot of fun.

Shit, look what we did to North Korea's missile program.

And then what Moscow pulled off in the 2016 American presidential election.

No, the internet ain't benign.

Hasn't gotten better in the last ten years. The 2022 market crash was ultimately traced to a Russian hack into the algorithms used for "dark pool trading." You know, the system where computers buy and trade thousands of shares based on minuscule changes in a stock's value—all within milliseconds, and far beyond the purview of the Security Exchange Commission. Seems the kids in Moscow figured out how to the game the system. In one week the Dow lost 23 percent of its value, at a pace just slow enough to avoid tripping the exchange auto cutoff mechanisms.

That sure as shit was no accident—and swung the midterms right into the Democrats' hands. The Republicans have been a shadow contender ever since.

Then we could talk about the German elections in 2023. Angela Merkel, a "Stone Queen" that "Iron Lady" Margret Thatcher would have admired, was chiseled to dust—dust, I'm telling you, dust—thanks to a wave of leaked emails and tawdry news stories concerning widespread bribery and corruption within the ranks of her party. All released one week before the election. No time for damage control.

I must admit the shit the Russians used to unseat Merkel was slick. They must have had a team of accountants, hackers, and novelists working 24/7 to push out that mountain of fake news in a way that fooled everyone—including NSA.

Which brings me up to the present, August 2025, another hot and sticky day here in the nation's capital. Not like I'm going for a run; the wheelchair gets me from point A to point B without having to jog. If I really want something, I go online and order it from Amazon. Even groceries are delivered in less than an hour now. Might take twelve hours for some of the stranger stuff, but no one goes to a mall anymore. Just let your fingers do the walking . . . sounds like one of those old Yellow Pages ads. Sorry, showing my age. Most of you have probably never seen a phone book; they stopped printing 'em years ago.

Normally, I'd be out at a rental on the Outer Banks, but staring at the waves gets old and I'm sick of the whole extended family gathering thing. They always shove me in a first-floor bedroom because it's "easier to access" and then I get to listen to the crowd bump around in the kitchen all morning. In this business work hours are, shall we say, "flexible." Makes me prone to work until 2:00 A.M. and get up around 10:00. Not rise and shine at 0630. Made staying home an easy decision.

Until Jared called—the CIA operations director.

Turns out we have new competition in making the world miserable.

Don't know who or where . . . or who they work for. Yet.

My job is to find out.

chapter 2

snake handler

montgomery, alabama, 15 august 2025

The seventy-two men came back in great joy. "Lord," they said, "even the demons obeyed us when we gave them a command in your name!" Jesus answered them, "I saw Satan fall like lightning from heaven. Listen! I have given you authority, so that you can walk on snakes and scorpions and overcome all the power of the Enemy, and nothing will hurt you."

—Luke 10:17-19

At age seventy-three, Vladimir Putin was on his twenty-sixth year of governing Russia and the Russians. Only Stalin had managed to survive as long—trudging ahead of his comrades from 1922 to 1953 (thirty-one years of misery) for himself and the nation. Russia is an ungovernable state. Spanning 5,700 miles and eleven time zones, the nation incorporates 185 ethnic groups with over a hundred languages outside of Russian itself.

Unmanageable. At least as a democracy.

Putin pretended to dictate via popular selection anyway. That, and his cadre of oligarchs. A collection of wealthy men who circled about the wealthiest man on earth… Putin. Estimated to be worth some

$84 billion. Not bad for a former KGB operative who proved of little value in the field, but understood Russian politics in a manner not witnessed since Peter the Great.

Lived by himself. Divorced these last eleven years. His two daughters were rarely in contact. Frankly, he found the solitude a blessing. The daily barrage of visitors and phone conversations left him exhausted, his legendary stamina now sapped by the passing of time. Not that aging deterred political ambitions. Vladimir Putin intended to remain in office until death called his name. Russia's new tsar.

He might even have been able to pull it off, save for the audacity of one Alexei Navalny.

Who'd been a pain in the ass since 2008. Started out by blogging, then began purchasing minority shares in major Russian corporations so that he could show up to meetings and ask embarrassing questions. Tossed into jail several times on embezzlement charges, the former lawyer managed to argue his way out. A campaign that caught international attention and restricted Putin's tendency to simply imprison his opposition.

At age forty-nine, Navalny had the ear of Russia's youth, and an ambition to steal Putin's thunder. While the old man pandered to church and mother Russia, Navalny was a true nationalist. He accused Putin of "sucking the blood out of Russia," and managed to launch a committee of academics, attorneys, and journalists to root out corruption—the source, he claimed, of money that enriched this new tsar and his circle of cronies.

Navalny was no fool.

The Cypriot banking crisis in 2012 had opened the door to a means of dispatching Putin. Turned out the Cypriots figured they could buy their way out of the bank collapse through a one-time tax on uninsured deposits totaling more than $100,000. With $60 billion in assets shelled away in Cyprus—the Mediterranean's version of a Caribbean tax shelter—the Russian oligarchs decided it was time to take their money and run.

Funny how the little things that fail to capture international attention often have inordinate significance.

Launched in 2009, Bitcoin, the first crypto currency, was valued at 7 cents a "coin." In August 2012, a "coin" was worth $13.31. By November 2012 it had fallen to $11 per "coin." And then on 25 March 2013, the day Cyprus was to begin its "bail-in" tax, a Bitcoin was suddenly worth $74. On 10 April 2013, a "coin" was selling for $181.

The Russian oligarchs had figured out how to move their money off Cyprus without paying the bank tax or having to file money transfer notifications.

Took Navalny and his team months to put all those pieces together. But now they knew. And, he suspected there was a means of "clawing back" a fair amount of that ill-begotten wealth. With Bitcoin now valued in the vicinity of $35,000 a coin, more than a few of Putin's *okruzheniya* (circle) kept a healthy chunk of their wealth in the crypto currency. Why not? More than five hundred thousand businesses worldwide accepted it as legal tender, and still no government had figured out how to tax the damn thing.

Navalny intended to get that money back and, in the process, strip the new tsar of his most valued supporters.

The trick was how.

That's where Adya Bakshi (literally "first paymaster" when translated from Hindi) came into the picture.

Ms. Bakshi—she preferred Dr. Bakshi—had a PhD in computer science and applied mathematics which *deserved* some recognition. Even if she had to pry it out of her male Indian counterparts. Damn Indian men—a collection of misogynist bastards who refused to join the twenty-first century.

Dr. Bakshi was an only child. Born and raised in Mumbai by a pair of college professors who were insistent their daughter was to become a doctor (the medical type) or engineer—both careers indicative of achieving the highest degree of success in Indian culture. She chose a more difficult course to the top—information technology—engineering via software.

As she would explain to her international counterparts at various business conferences, to get into a computer science program at a prestigious Indian university, one had to be at the top of one's secondary school class, master the "Joint Entrance Examination – Advanced," then pray one was in the .92 percent of applicants who were actually admitted to one of the Indian Institutes of Technology.

She not only got in on the first try, the "old boys' club" kept her on to finish a doctorate. Followed by a two-year post-doctorate appointment to MIT.

But designing new chips was not her thing. For Dr. Bakshi it was all about programming. And not for industry—too mundane.

Her step into the dark world came at the 2018 DEF CON. Held in Las Vegas on an annual basis, DEF CON is the world's largest gathering of hackers—black hat (the bad guys) and white hat (the good guys)—all assembled to discuss the latest escapades, new code vulnerabilities, and look for work. It wasn't unusual for the director of the National Security Agency to make an appearance, and CIA kept a small cadre of recruiters circling the various sessions.

Bakshi also had no, zero, interest in working for Uncle Sam or any other government. Nor was she initially enticed by the dark side collective—yes, there were DEF CON attendees looking to employ persons willing to steal identities, hack into corporate networks to steal intellectual property, and even subvert the Society for Worldwide Interbank Financial Telecommunication (SWIFT) transaction system, the means by which banks securely transferred funds from one account to another anywhere on the planet (she figured the SWIFT job offer was a joke, until someone quietly noted that Pyongyang had managed to pull off its electronic heist of $81 million from a bank in Bangladesh only by hiring at DEF CON.)

She had to admit the money offers coming from the dark side were intriguing. Her parents were not wealthy, and could use the funds to retire to southern India, perhaps even to Mysore; it was supposed to be clean, quiet, and easy to reach.

It was a pair of young kids who lured her in.

Probably no older than twenty-five, the two approached her at the end of day three. She'd asked a number of probing questions during a small break-off session on router access options—as in routers for "cloud computing centers." After hackers discovered backdoors into Huawei's systems in 2017, all the giant data storage centers became fair game. Amazon spent more money and time on cyber security campaigns than it did on updating its customer interface or web pages. Had to. The class-action lawsuit concerning identity theft and purloined credit card numbers in 2021 removed a tidy $25 billion from Jeff Bezos's bottom line. That's what happens when you own the world's largest online retail service.

In any case, she'd asked the right questions.

And gave better answers then the presenters.

One week later, Dr. Bakshi found an apartment in Montgomery, Alabama. Her new business partners liked the city, and she found the climate similar to home. In this line of work it really didn't matter where you lived. Montgomery just happened to be cheap, civilized, and an easy commute to Atlanta should they need to travel internationally at a reasonable price. She missed home, but was weary of India's crowds, limited employment opportunities, and sexism.

Their first target was fascinating—access Google's search engine and make changes that caused her new client's advertisements to pop up on the top of every search—*without* paying Google for the privilege.

It took the three of them one month to pull it off without alerting the search giant's security forces.

For one glorious week they managed to hold Google at bay. Their client made a shitload of money. Her team got its first bonus.

From there it was on to servicing a customer who wanted his competitor's goods delisted on Amazon. A neat trick. Took

Amazon forty-three days to fix that problem. Another payoff for the "Montgomery Mafia"—that's what they began calling themselves.

Even advertised their services on the dark web—used Dream Market.

The first job culled from that was a drop into HP—"borrowing" the latest 3-D printer designs for a client in Taiwan.

The second one found them planting email prior to a corporate board meeting concerning selection of a new CEO. The bastard who hired them won the position soon after the board members were delivered a sequence of messages concerning the myriad sexual indiscretions of his competitors.

The third big job—there was always a slew of minor crap that people requested, screw up Facebook pages, forward all my neighbor's email to another account, lower all utility bills for a client's business—was more daunting. A dark website requesting placement of "news" stories obviously intended to derail the career of a certain congressman in California.

"Why use the dark web?" Dr. Bakshi asked one of her new colleagues.

"Social media is too obvious. This way the news jackals will stumble onto the story and start firing rumor and innuendo without having a traceable account or URL," they'd replied.

"We can do that via Facebook." Her retort.

"Let some poor bastard on the dark web take the fall—*we* stay in business."

She agreed. And went to work . . . only to realize the site in question was running out of a server in Russia, and that every one of her key strokes was obviously being recorded.

To make things more disconcerting, the site's administrator was likely following her infiltration as a silent bloodhound. She would select a directory tree to hit a selected file path and then on the next keystroke get this sensation of someone breathing down her virtual neck.

Very creepy. Had never happened before.

Her cell phone rang just before the first page of propaganda was being slotted for posting. A buzz that caused the good doctor to startle. The timing was obviously not coincidental. No number displayed on the screen. She ignored the phone; it kept ringing. Strange, should've gone directly to voicemail.

Buzz number fifteen caused her to pick up the damn thing and answer.

"I see you work in politics." An accent any movie fan would immediately identify as Russian.

"Who is this?" Her tentative response—*this* had never happened before.

"Perhaps, I shall ask the questions, since *you're* on *my* fucking web page." Still came through as a threat, despite the bad connection.

This guy had not only traced her movements online, he also had access to some database that spit out what had previously been an unlisted number. Probably had her home address by now. For a moment she contemplated flight. Too late.

"Want to stay in business?"

"Yes." A slight quiver in her voice. Hopefully the shitty connection would mask the sound of her fear.

"Get the fuck off my web page. Answer my next call immediately. Two days." The connection cut out.

Deep breath. Deep breath.

She called her second "business partner."

"I'm going to bypass Facebook's source tracking code and put this political shit on the congressman's Facebook page."

Long pause on the other side. "You sure you can do that? What happened to our original plan?"

She thought about explaining, but knew better. At least on a phone. If the Russian bastard had found her that quickly, he likely was now tapped into her telecommunications.

An accurate assessment.

Fedor Ivanov was now recording everything that went through Dr. Bakshi's iPhone—blame Apple, they never patched the Spectre backdoor. Claimed it would slow devices down to a point customers would bitch. Plus, the kids in Silicon Valley argued, the Spectre vulnerability was too hard to access for *any* random hacker.

Except Fedor was no *random* hacker. He was one of the best in the business. Why do you think we all got to read Hillary Clinton's email?

"I can do it . . . trust me." She hung up.

The California congressman was front-page news the next day.

And there was no knock on their door. They stayed in business. Paid handsomely by a "nonprofit" 501C3 operating out of a sweet set of offices on K Street in downtown Washington, DC. Facebook never knew what hit them.

It was the call that came twenty-four hours later when Dr. Bakshi began to realize the future was more complicated than she had anticipated.

She'd been ultra-cautious—that IT education included a large collection of cyber security classes and a number of hard-learned lessons (like the time one of her classmates turned on the camera in her laptop and then displayed Bakshi naked and showering before an audience of his peers. Thank god he hadn't posted it to the internet. And that her father had some friends who came down to the university and beat the shit out of the young man in question, smashing his computer in the process—what a shame).

In her caution, the old phone—a brand-new iPhone XII—had been tossed into a nearby river. She'd purchased a Huawei V and changed service providers and telephone numbers.

And still he found her.

"Being difficult, or just paranoid?" His idea of an opening introduction.

"Being careful." Her Indian lilt on the English language came across as quite pronounced, which always happened when she was nervous.

"You are going to do some work for us, when I ask. The answer to that statement is yes. Understand?"

Dr. Bakshi took a deep breath. "Yes."

"Good. I'd hate to have you looking for a new job or spending time in jail. The FBI does not smile on such activities as you and your friends are engaged in. I'll call you when we are in need. Until then, stay off my web page."

The call was over.

She zapped an email to her two twenty-something partners. "Need to meet for dinner. Let's gather at India Palace . . . 7:30 this evening."

Took more than a little explaining, but the partnership didn't end. They just never spoke more than a casual greeting on any phone. Email exchanges among the three had always been abstract—now they became runic. If you live to hack, you know you will be hacked.

Meanwhile the Facebook backdoor took on a life of its own. Suddenly, they had more political customers than one could imagine. Seems the politicos figured out it was more effective to covertly imbed their messages—largely attack stories and sordid sexual tales on a thousand Facebook pages—than it was to purchase advertising or speak off the record with a local reporter. What social media giveth, social media taketh away. Which more than paid for her parents' new flat in Mysore.

Life was good.

Until Fedor called Dr. Bakshi again, this time with Alexei Navalny on speakerphone.

chapter 3

loose ends

moscow, russia, 16 august 2025

At age thirty-six, Fedor Ivanov was, physically, your standard Russian male. Years of a poor diet, too much vodka, and a two-pack-a-day smoking habit had left him thirty pounds overweight with a phlegmy cough. His skin had a pallor most Americans associated with a corpse lying in a casket. Not much exposure to sunlight when you make a living hacking into other people's networks. That, and Moscow was never a place to work on your tan.

He lived alone. Had tried dating on several occasions, but his work hours—and lack of social skills—condemned him to imagined encounters with the opposite sex while he perused an online porn site. He was not the man of any Russian woman's dreams.

However, he was also not your typical hacker slob.

His apartment in the Patriarchy Prudy—close to Patriarchy Pond—was a two-bedroom masterpiece. The building had been constructed in 1873. Intended for embassy staffers seeking lodging close to work, it featured marble floors, large windows, and a fireplace. The kitchen had been remodeled in 2017, leaving him with granite countertops and all stainless-steel appliances. Not that he was much of a cook.

Furnishing for everything but his office (the second bedroom) came from shuttered Russian estates. He'd haunted antique dealers for over three years before reaching a point of satisfaction. In contrast to the furniture, the art was all best described as "modern." No famous names, but there were huge splashes of color across every wall. Helped offset the gray winters.

The office was a complete change of pace. He'd paid an electrician to run lines sufficient to power 50-inch TVs mounted on all four walls—every one of them visible from his desk. The floor was carpeted with a Turkish rug that allowed him to scoot about in a wheeled ergo chair. He'd gone to basic black for the furnishings. There was no ceiling light—any illumination aside from the three computer screens on his desk and four television screens came from LED lamps placed below eyelevel. The curtains were always closed.

It was the perfect hacker's cavern. However, instead of a litter of pizza boxes and over-filled ashtrays, it was spotless. Just like the rest of the apartment. One of his associates, upon coming to visit, declared Fedor was anal retentive. He didn't argue or disagree (guilty as charged).

What his associate failed to notice was the server rack and stack of blinking equipment Fedor kept behind a locked closet door. He had enough storage to hold ten petabytes of data (by comparison, the U.S. Library of Congress is estimated to have about fifteen terabytes of information in its entire holdings).

He could, if necessary, pull down and store all the digital holdings resident in any major corporation around the globe. A handy option when you steal all their files and then issue ransom demands. Which paid his bills on a regular basis.

Not terribly difficult to accomplish. Even after thirty years of exposure to internet intrusions, many companies still lacked sophisticated firewalls and a security-conscious staff. The folks in most corporate accounting offices had convinced management it was cheaper to risk a bit of cyber hacking than to impede overall productivity. Usually, the accountants were right. But there were examples of significant intellectual property being sold to competitors based on an offer from the highest bidder.

That's where the third computer on Fedor's desk came into play. Working through "the onion router" (Tor) he ran his own dark website that was a marketplace for purloined intellectual property ranging from designs for fuel-efficient engines to all the source code necessary to operate a 5G telephone network. Only accepted pay in Bitcoin—cash was too risky. And he never offered an identity—in fact, he had no hacker name at all.

That said, his website—Endless Horizons—was well known and frequently drew press attention after a corporation would announce penetration of a particularly valuable database. He managed to fend off law enforcement, other hackers, and industrial cyber security specialists via employment of his own coding methods and the configuration of eight routers that left no URL footprint behind.

Until that damn Indian woman had crept in, messing up his artfully arranged world.

He would have missed Dr. Bakshi's intrusion entirely had he not been engaged in vetting a sequence of bids on a data base for satellite designs he had "borrowed" from Raytheon. Fedor was shocked with the ease she demonstrated in bypassing his firewalls and then navigating through a set of security programs he had personally written and never marketed. The woman was good, damn good. She only set off his alert system—a set of electronic trip wires—when the file she was trying to implant on his website failed to pass through a screening code he had installed less than a week prior.

In other words, he got lucky.

Took a little effort to track down her phone and disable the controls. Catching her move to a new cell was a lot easier; he had access to every phone company data base and new device tracking system. In layman's terms, he simply traced the URL for the corporate entity providing her access to the internet, then he geolocated the server, and then began screening for new phone additions at nearby points of sale.

The first time he tried this stunt it took him twelve hours. By the time he met Dr. Bakshi, he could pull it off within about thirty minutes of a phone being activated. Wrote his own algorithms to accomplish the feat—didn't share them with the hacking world.

Fedor's single weakness, aside from his failure to exercise and quit smoking, was a nearly psychotic hatred for Vladimir Putin. Raised by a single father who had managed to succeed in climbing the Foreign Intelligence Service of the Russian Federation (SVR) bureaucratic ranks, the man insisted his son get a good education and attempted to avoid the corruption and political favoritism endemic in any major government agency operating out of Moscow. He'd succeeded in getting Fedor into the right schools, but failed at avoiding the consequences of enraging the new circle of wealthy oligarchs. Well-intentioned men seldom survive... the Bible was wrong, the meek shall not inherit the earth.

It was only after Fedor graduated from college and embarked on his career in hacking that he discovered his father's fate. The man had disappeared—entirely—during Fedor's senior year in high school. No one would tell him why. When he pushed the issue, a policeman came by the school to claim his father likely had been drunk and fallen off a bridge into the river.

Complete bullshit.

Thanks to lousy IT services, the SVR systems were still vulnerable. What Fedor found in them left a permanent animosity for Putin. His father had been murdered by a security detail assigned to one of Putin's closest allies. Seems *Otets* (father) had caught the man in the process of lining his own pockets by directing profits from a state-owned oil company into private accounts in the Caribbean. Threatened to make the theft public during Putin's third run for the Russian presidency.

Otmshcheniye.

Fedor pledged to avenge the murder.

Step one had been to bankrupt the oligarch by cleaning out his bank accounts. Fedor donated all the cash to charities.

Step two was to get Putin—a far more difficult task. The man walled himself off physically and electronically.

So, Fedor went in search of Putin's political opponents—and landed up in Alexi Navalny's office . . . in November 2023.

Navalny listened, but said nothing. He too knew the risks of fucking with Vladimir Putin. It took two weeks of conversation and Fedor's demonstrated ability to steal political secrets and plant unfavorable stories without detection before Navalny began to trust the young computer nerd.

By now the two men were a close team—Navalny was its very public face, while Fedor worked behind the scenes.

Made for interesting times. Putin's advance teams would show up for a political event, only to find a collection of demonstrators outfitted with colorful signs decrying the new tsar. They often had witty slogans and even more interesting chants. And then there were the slew of YouTube videos and music ballads, all aimed at insulting the Russian president.

No one took credit for the work, it just launched into the ether.

Fedor was going to make Navalny—the wayward lawyer—Putin's successor.

Maybe.

Vladimir Putin did not rise from the KGB to the Kremlin because he was blessed. The emergence from political exile in East Germany happened as a result of "unfortunate" bad fish his ex-wife used to poison Vladimir's adversaries at a sequence of "meetings" he held in his house. Passed off as "Soviet Salons," the meetings were a means of identifying friends and foes. Friends were fine the day after, foes landed up with the "flu" for weeks. Botulism is an ugly thing. Putin blamed it on the water supply. His wife knew better—a bottle of pills in the house marked "antacid" were actually penicillin, clindamycin, and cephalosporins. The latter two caused diarrhea and dehydration. The East German doctors never figured it out. Sent the Putins' guests home to mother Russia instead. The East German doctors didn't want the messy politics of a dead Russian on their hands.

Thirty years later, Putin was not about to put up with this internet bullshit. His security team went into a full-court press in hopes of hunting down the guilty party. To no avail. They started with the known Russian hacker community, then migrated to targeted searches of various server sites.

No luck.

That led to selective arrests and long interrogation sessions.

Fedor was a lone operator. No one to squeal if the heat turned up.

Then Navalny was hauled in. Once, twice, three times.

Beat the shit out of him. Emerged from prison and called Fedor for a meeting. Give the man credit, he had two black eyes and a broken nose. Also managed to lose ten pounds in the course of a month. Apparently Russian prison food did not agree with his digestive system.

Never mentioned Fedor's name despite the abuse.

A hard way to earn loyalty, but he succeeded. Fedor would drop everything at a phone call from Navalny.

Well, not everything.

Endless Horizons grew from a site trafficking in stolen intellectual property to a one-stop shopping market for assassination, "borrowed" antique automobiles, credit cards (at least the numbers lifted from transactions), porn, narcotics, and weapons. Profits flitted between $17 and $25 million a year. Paid for his apartment, then the 2019 Mercedes G-Class SUV.

Those expenditures were his extravagances; the remainder went to meeting daily expenses and a healthy savings account parked in a U.S. bank. He was willing to pay the taxes in exchange for a guarantee his money was secure. No Panama Papers were going to divulge his holdings.

The one thing Fedor couldn't bear was the idea of leaving Russia. His English was marginal. His German was little better. So, he took the chance of being rounded up.

Two attempts at hacking into any one of the three computers in his office would cause the machine to lock down—permanently. The hard drive wipe and anything in the random access memory (RAM) was toast. An approach that could be expensive, but he could afford replacements. He could not envision time in a prison cell. Besides, the backup sat in cloud storage provided by an Amazon computing center located just outside Fargo, North Dakota.

He was digitally courageous, but not stupid.

A path that proved all too wise when Navalny went to jail for the fourth time in less than eighteen months. Putin's goons were not playing games this time. Broke both of the man's legs and then started pulling out fingernails.

Shortly thereafter came a knocking on Fedor's front door. Polite, but insistent.

They had no warrant and wore no uniforms. Didn't break anything. Just walked off with his laptops. He wisely offered no protest. Machines were easy to purchase.

Didn't surprise him when the same goons returned three days later. This time they were more intrusive. He would have used the word "angry" if one of the neighbors asked—they didn't.

Took his replacement systems away, punched him in the face a few times, and threatened to seize his holdings if they could not get into the new machines. They could. He was not so foolish as to deny the Putin security buffoons a look at his work a second time. The trick was content. There was no mention of Endless Horizons, nor was there any indication of his programming skills on the machines they seized, just three boxes loaded with standard Microsoft setups and a bit of innocuous material—innocent photos and letters to supposed friends.

It worked. There was no third "visit."

Navalny went home to his wife and children. Then they resumed planting nasty rumors about President Putin and his circle of oligarchs. With Fedor dedicated to extensive research.

Locations for the secret prisons were released online. Then came a selective trickle of stories on the various investments and dubious business deals. Followed by news reports of tax dodging and political favors. And spreadsheets revealing Putin's wealth.

Scandals that would have ended a congressional career in the United States.

Shrugged off in Russia.

Russians were used to political malfeasance. Shit, the last 100 years of Russian history was nothing but political malfeasance. Perhaps it would be more accurate to say the last 150 years of Russian history was nothing but political malfeasance. From Tsar Nicholas II to Lenin, Stalin, Brezhnev, and now Putin, the Kremlin was little more than a home for shameless thieves. All stealing from the pockets of common men and women.

Fedor seethed at the thought. He'd inherited his father's passion for political honesty, but lacked his courage.

At least physical courage.

Fedor opted to stay in the shadows. Let the professional politician—Navalny—carry the weight of battling Putin's ambitions in the public forum. He had to admit Navalny was a brave man. Opinion polls revealed Putin was a popular figure even among millennials and Generation Z. The bastard was getting old, but the twenty-somethings still supported him. Toppling this regime was going to take more than rumors and evidence of widespread theft of public property.

Fedor hoped it was coming with the arrival of Dr. Bakshi.

chapter 4

it's all uphill in the snow from here

washington, dc, 18 august 2025

Strikes me that I've made no introductions. Typical computer geek, stare at the screen and forget social niceties like an exchange of names. Momma named me Tiana. Dad called me Toad. My friends issued me a new call sign after my accident—Roller. Kind of like the last one, evokes my motorcycle days and describes the wheelchair driver I've become.

That's what you can call me—Roller. Anything else and I shut off your electricity.

Been a slow couple of weeks. Family came back from the Outer Banks and promptly invaded my house. I live a block off Independence Avenue, quiet neighborhood with a view of the Capitol Building—it's less than half a mile away. Easy rolling distance to Eastern Market. Surrounded by white families with kids—the black folks got priced out fifteen years ago.

Makes me a target for attention. African-American woman with a wheelchair lift instead of steps for a front entrance. Oh, I left some space on the front steps—the door is ten feet above ground level—wouldn't be polite to make guests have to wander through the alley and come in via a back door. Reeks of the kind of shit they did with "colored" help back in the 1950s.

My parents like my town house. I live on the first floor and they get the second level as guest quarters. Just wish they'd leave the grandkids my brother produced at home. Damn crumb-snatchers burn up internet access—slows down my work, while they sit and play the latest online silliness.

Well, it's just for a few days. And it's nice to have the distraction.

Pardon the bad pun, meals turn into freewheeling events when the folks come to stay. I hear about everything from cousins still living in North Carolina to my father's latest investment tips (he's made a small fortune in the stock market). Mom taught school—DC public schools no less. But they chose to live in Silver Springs, Maryland. She'd jump on the Metro for a ride to downtown, he'd go to Union Station and catch the train for New York. Stayed for the week and came back late on Friday night. They pulled that off for thirty years. Made for a good marriage. Absence and occupation make the heart grow fonder.

Not sure their two children helped with that. My brother and I were a genuine pain in Mom's ass. Behaved like saints when Dad was home. He grew up in the back hills of North Carolina—a belt was still considered an appropriate means of disciplining wayward offspring. He took that to heart... as my brother and I both discovered. Mom resorted to verbal lectures. Guess it was the elementary school teacher coming out in her.

I climbed into the digital world in Montgomery Blair High School; only black female in the cyber classes they offered. Listen, you little shit, that was twenty years ago, girls didn't do programming. *Black* girls sure as shit didn't do programming—but *I* did.

Went to school at the University of Maryland. A short bus ride from home. Mom liked having my company, tuition was reasonable, Dad kept pulling in the bucks. All good. My damn baby brother was the problem.

Went to the Naval Academy, then into the Marine Corps as a 2nd lieutenant. Said he didn't want to be "stuck on a ship." Why the fuck would you go to the Naval Academy if you didn't want to be at sea? Well, the Marine Corps solved that problem. Sent him to Iraq twice and Afghanistan—four times.

With that track record we were all surprised when he came home to announce he was engaged. To a white girl who ran a nonprofit in DC. She chased environmental issues, he specialized in destroying the landscape. Go figure.

Had their first child after year three years. Second one came eighteen months later. Bro found a job in DC running down issues law enforcement could not resolve. Still wears the Marine uniform on reserve drill weekends. Moved the family into a house two blocks from me after my motorcycle accident. Comes by to help with repairs and gardening. Sends the kids over to make sure I'm behaving and making meals. All good shit.

Except he wouldn't tell me what *really* pays his bills.

(I found that out through a digital backdoor, but that story can wait. Trust me, we *will* be revisiting the nature of his occupation.)

Me. Well, after college I took a job with Microsoft. Found a rental on Mercer Island in Seattle. Writing code for what became Bill Gates's first stab at providing cyber security for the Windows operating system. It was a crash course in working endless hours on a tight deadline. My team pulled it off for three weeks of unmitigated success. Then I caught an intrusion on a machine at about 0330 one morning. Told you I don't sleep at night.

Took a while to figure out where they were crawling in. Classic zero day break-in.

I should probably explain that.

All software, I don't care how damn good you think it is, has holes in it. Exploitable gaps that someone—usually with untoward intentions—discovers and exploits until the software provider discovers the problem and "patches" the hole. The day on which a hacker discovers the problem is "zero day."

Turns out our intelligence community has an agreement with the software gurus. The kids at NSA will help patch a hole, but only *after* seven days of access. What the bad guys exploit, the "good" guys also employ. So, Facebook, Google, and Microsoft all agree to inform NSA and CYBERCOM when they discover a zero day defect and plan to plug the leak. Gives the intel types a week of further collection—if, if they've already discovered this latest "backdoor."

Trust me, they find the backdoors. And rarely inform the provider. Unless it's a glaring deficiency or they are watching some adversary rape government computers with impunity.

When it's *their* secrets walking off it's all hands on deck. If it's anyone bleeding data that might serve the intel community... too fucking bad. Two-faced bastards.

Back to my story. It's 0330 in 2019 and I'm watching a mole creep through our software and begin ransacking Microsoft servers for files associated with a planned rewrite of the Outlook mail programs. Only they aren't pulling the kind of files one would expect—design, delivery, efficiency—they're going through the code intended to ensure *privacy*. In other words, how to break into Outlook without alerting users or the system administrators. Clever.

Persistent bastards. Kept stripping off files for forty-five minutes. Then "quietly" backed out.

By then I had a pretty good fix on their server locale.

Fort Meade.

Didn't say anything to my boss the next morning.

Did exactly what we were told not to do at Microsoft; sent a mole of my own up the same path the intruder employed. Put in the right code and you can leave a message—a URL for a server in my house with a damn good firewall. Kind of like writing graffiti intended to draw a response. The reader has to interpret the scrawl and know how to place the letters in context so as to connect it with a person.

Took my target seventy-four hours.

Then he, or she—never found out—hit me back a response: "Want a job?"

Thought long and hard about that for twenty-four hours. I liked Seattle, but missed my family. I liked Microsoft, but felt like just another cog in Bill Gates's profit monster. Why not go do something for national security?

Money.

Fucking government likes to lowball potential employees. First offer came in $35,000 a year below what I was earning at Microsoft. At that rate I'd be back to living at home and listening to Mom's lectures. No thanks. I love my mother, but at twenty-eight I wasn't ready to resume abiding by her rules and tutelage.

I countered (mind you this is all taking place through a zero-day defect in my then-employer's software) for five grand over what Gates and company were paying me at the time.

Turns out audacity is not without virtue. NSA coughed up the cash.

Convinced my dad to take a week off and drive back across country with me. Pulling a rented U-Haul trailer full of my worldly possessions. Arrived in DC with all my savings from Microsoft and went house shopping. That's how I landed up on Capitol Hill. I owned the shittiest house with no furnishings. Slept on a futon for months.

But, little by little, it all came together.

After going through the new employee bullshit, I was assigned to TAO. And was told I could work from home. My targets were all unclassified machines scattered across the planet.

Anyone who grants you that license—the work-from-home thing, DC commuting royally sucks—is my hero. Did NSA's bidding for three years. Then I got a call from a CIA recruiter. Yes, yes, I know—going to work for the agency that really does kill people. NSA was just stuck with that stereotype in the movies—the geeks at Fort Meade wouldn't know which end of the gun to point at a target. Might be able to disconnect their intended victim's internet access, but kill them? Not in the foreseeable future.

CIA, the ever-immodest organization, never liked being beholden to other members of the intelligence community. Yes, NSA is a giant organization that specializes in communications and signals intercepts, but CIA maintains its own operation with similar capabilities. Same thing when it comes to imagery or analysis. Shit, the Agency even has its own small army of operatives culled from the various military services. One-stop shopping for a White House that wants to avoid drawing attention to its needs and desires.

Given all that capability you'd think the boys at Langley would be all over protecting their own IT systems. You'd be wrong. I walked in and discovered a software rat's nest of patches and failed coordination among the system admin types. They knew the Agency was a target for every hacker looking to win bragging rights. And more than a few foreign governments in search of Washington's darkest secrets.

No surprise in either case, but the absence of a concerted defense, particularly on the Agency's unclassified network, was appalling. Just the kind of challenge a newly promoted GS-15 like me was seeking. Plugging in with a talent pool that would have made Microsoft jealous, we not only shut the backdoors, we even launched a campaign to kick in the front doors.

Started with our own bosses. Working out of the house, I'd figured out the path to access, read and write the CIA director's unclassified email. Just to prove it could be done, I composed a set of messages for his chief of information operations (CIO). Expressed concern with the CIO's lack of progress on the offensive side and pointed out continuing disappointment with the quality of CIA cyber defenses. That went on for a week until I came clean with the CIO—my top manager—and suggested he contact Microsoft about the zero-day hole I was using to make his life miserable.

Funny thing, the CIA's top cheese never figured out I was hacking his email. Too busy sucking dick down at the White House to pay attention to the sent email box on his own machine. Makes you wonder how some of these top folks survive in the modern world.

Be careful what you ask for. The CIO took to heart my push for an offensive front. Only he wanted to do it via AI. Yeah, the scary stuff you see in the movies right before the robots take over and we humans get shuffled off to prison camps or snuffed.

I can tell you right now, AI ain't close to being that good. Going to be a long time before a set of algorithms replaces *my* coding skills. That, and we do pretty well in adapting to completely unexpected developments. Still not the case with "smart" devices.

However, and this is a big however, you *can* put some code together that will learn to crawl around deep recesses of the internet and seek out access points on intended targets' networks or personal machines—including their "smart" vehicles, the kind that come with four wheels. This AI tries one mode of access, when that doesn't work it switches to another approach, when that doesn't work it takes a third approach, and so on, until it gets in and sends us a note that the following data is now available. All the while it's "learning" new software access tricks.

Gets to the point where some of the AI "crawlers" can cut through the security walls in seconds. Those are the real smart ones. The dumb AI is called "weeds." They just jam up the internet. Good for denial of service attacks, bad if you need high speed and actual access to an adversary's information. The "weeds" are a nuisance and there are a lot of them. Another problem with AI—fucking programs like to "breed," creating more "weeds."

AI "weeds" reached a point a few years ago that caused the rich and famous who attend Davos—you know, that gathering of business and political elites in Switzerland at the height of ski season—to spend a whole day discussing the fate of their beloved World Wide Web.

Talk, talk, talk. No action. What were they going to do? Establish a completely neutral body to babysit the internet? Either we, NSA, or the black-hat hackers would have shut that shit down in less than twenty-four hours. To say nothing of how the Russians and Chinese would have reacted.

Trust me, baby, the cyber world is a disaster waiting to happen. Often with no means of assigning attribution. Chinese tried. Put up the "Great Wall" software barrier around their internet connections.

Estonians, Israelis, and Russians attempted the same thing. All "walls" do is attract raiders—there *must* be something valuable behind that defensive barrier—attack! Turned it into an online game in the black-hat world. Winners paid in Bitcoin.

Proof of entry? A digital spray-painting of the "offending" country's cyber security offices' websites and then a public release of the software used to maintain their "wall."

Was a real popular game in the black-hat world, until the Russians started physically hunting down the offenders and cutting off hands. Only cost you one the first time. Offend twice, you lost both hands. The dead tell no tales—or so the pirates used to claim—amputees can spread word of impending disaster.

Trust me, word got out fast.

Until *we* started hunting the Russian hit teams. Two can play at that game. Sent pictures back to Moscow with the noose already around their necks. Told you, I went to work for the one agency that can permanently solve problems.

Unfortunately, the Russians weren't the only ones who responded to cyber warfare with physical violence. The Chinese went after their domestic offenders with grim determination. One day the suspect was online, the next he or she was not, ever again.

As for Washington, well, the last Republican administration redrafted U.S. nuclear strategy and very publicly announced any effort to use cyber weapons as a means of destroying the nation's power grid or communications nodes would warrant first use of a nuclear device.

Shit, that's a precedent no one wants to set, and yet, there it was in the current Nuclear Posture Review. Boys in the Pentagon signed off on the document, as did the White House.

Now the bits and bytes came with an offer of annihilation.

Didn't stop the hackers, and sure as hell didn't close down *my* office. We just learned to be even more subtle. Fuck that "turn things off" campaign, we set about changing realities.

Catch me if you can.

chapter

5

freedom is not free . . . some strings are attached

moscow, russia, 20 august 2025

We must be staunch in our conviction that freedom is not the sole prerogative of a lucky few but the inalienable and universal right of all human beings.

—Ronald Reagan, 1982

Navalny bought into Reagan's dream. A vision of untrammeled electorates announced before the British Parliament in that temple of democracy, Westminster Abbey.

Reagan's words gave birth to the National Endowment for Democracy—via U.S. congressional dictate—and then a pair of shadowy organizations that drew less attention, but supposedly were dedicated to promoting rule of the people for the people.

Think of it this way, the National Endowment for Democracy is funded via an annual appropriation from the U.S. budget and is subject to congressional oversight. Not surprisingly, given its purported mission—promoting democracy abroad—members of the NED are not welcome in a fair number of countries, including Russia. However, two organizations that manage—mysteriously—to draw significantly less press attention often send representatives into places the NED teams cannot enter.

Those two would be the International Republican Institute (IRI) and the National Democratic Institute (NDI). Both of these institutes claim to be nonpartisan, but, as their names and boards of directors make clear, have very close ties to the two major American political parties. And dubious histories. IRI is infamous for training the men who staged a coup in Haiti in 2004 and then setting up support for the 2009 Honduran coup d'état. And then funding the development of conservative think tanks in Honduras and Mexico. Oh, not insignificantly, it also helped corral conservative parties in Poland who then compelled the formation of a coalition government from 1997 to 2001.

For some reason, IRI had yet to draw Putin's ire, so they were allowed a footprint in Moscow.

NDI was less controversial, but had developed a reputation for employing its goals of "democracy assistance" and "democracy building" to disrupt nationalist and socialist movements that protest American economic and cultural imperialism. NDI had been tossed out of Russia back in 2012 and Cambodia in 2017. So, instead of an office in Moscow, NDI funneled money into anti-Putin movements via Bitcoin—and provided online training for self-proclaimed democracy activists.

Like Navalny.

Strangely, he never heard from anyone at CIA. That bastion of anti-authoritarianism, according to the employees of said Agency. Salvador Allende, Fidel Castro, or Saddam Hussein might offer concurring opinions.

There was a good explanation for CIA's absence—Iraq, 2003.

The Agency first got burned by "Curveball" on the mobile chemical weapons assessment, then it got worse. Ahmed Chalabi, the Shia businessman and politician who drove America into a war. Back in 1992 his bank in Jordan failed to the tune of a $350 million bailout from Amman. He pushed a failed insurrection in northern Iraq in 1995, fled to the United States, and managed to bilk $100 million from American tax payers via congressional support for his political party. Had nearly unfettered access to CIA. Never amounted to anything in the post-Saddam regimes.

Curveball and Chalabi made CIA more than a little reluctant to reach into some nascent political "revolution." The boys at Langley stayed away from the Arab Spring in 2011 like a beaten dog. And knew better than to mess with Putin. Once a spook, always a spook. Putin kept a heavy hand on the CIA presence in Russia.

Which left Navalny dangling in the wind.

Save his access to IRI via Tor.

"The onion router," a relatively secure means of communications for those who would topple governments Washington preferred to see depart. Works like this—Tor is a network built atop the internet. It separates the user's identification from the routes employed to move their packets of data (the collection of bits and bytes chopped up and then rebundled when you send information across the internet). This "onion routing" uses multilayered encryption (hence the "onion" label) across more than seven thousand relays provided by volunteers at locales scattered around the globe. Using the standard internet, it's possible to geolocate a sender and receiver. Tor takes that option away and (supposedly) has remained secure for the last twenty-three years.

Here's the kicker—Tor began at the U.S. Naval Research Laboratory in the mid-nineties and then was picked up by the Defense Advanced Research Projects Agency (DARPA) in 1997. To this day, the Pentagon and State Department pay for almost all maintenance and upgrade costs.

Slower than the everyday internet, but prevented one's being arrested for political indiscretions. And, inadvertently, abetted crime. The dark web sales sites all employed Tor.

Including Fedor's Endless Horizons. A development the boys at State hadn't anticipated—but DARPA should have, shit, they were trying to develop a means of securing U.S. intelligence community communications. If it's good enough for the intel agencies, it should work for organized crime.

Navalny could not have cared less about all this technical crap. Fedor had tried to explain the system multiple times, but Navalny just nodded his head and continued with his emails to IRI. Fuck, he was a lawyer and politician, not some fucking computer geek. That was Fedor's role in their relationship. As Navalny once told Fedor when the younger man was on a roll concerning IT systems, "Just tell me the time, don't explain the damn clock."

IRI was a font of good ideas, but generates little money. Navalny figured the IRI office was being fed by members of the U.S. intelligence community. How else would they *know* all the stories and banking data that came into his email? He'd asked Fedor to check more than a few emails for accuracy. The hacker never came back with a negative response. Which left Navalny worried he was just a tool for the U.S. government. A tool that could be abandoned on the street if the job became too demanding or dangerous.

He didn't sleep well at night.

Didn't help being the "unicorn" of contemporary Russian politics. He'd opened the Anti-Corruption Foundation back in 2011. Targeting the oligarchs surrounding Putin. Just asking for personal disaster, or so his friends liked to tell Navalny. Was arrested, tried, and jailed in 2013 for embezzlement. Sentenced to five years in prison, he was back out on the streets in twenty-four hours.

In December 2015, his team released a YouTube documentary revealing extensive ties between the Russian prosecutor general and the country's most violent organized crime families. Claimed the prosecutor was worth billions—a sum impossible to acquire on a government salary. Was of course denounced as an American plot to besmirch Putin's administration. Almost nothing happened to Navalny, even though the YouTube clip drew over a million views in less than forty-eight hours of release.

Was put on house arrest and shackled with a surveillance bracelet. He cut it off and went back to wandering the streets, attending to his business and political events. The police ignored his noncompliance.

Instead, the Russian authorities tried to muzzle him by arresting his brother. Jailed the younger sibling. Navalny ignored the flagrant blackmail. Denounced the move as a tactic picked up from Stalin. Didn't curtail his political activities (pictures of his sibling posted above Navalny's desk, however, reveal the toll prison has taken on his brother—aged thirty years in less than ten behind bars).

Went on to run for mayor of Moscow in 2020. Despite the obvious manipulations carried out by Putin's team, he managed to pull down 42 percent of the popular vote. Young, educated Russians loved him. The establishment was ready to have him killed.

With all that in mind, this latest development left Navalny completely sleepless.

IRI's most recent email: "We recommend a selected campaign targeting a few members of Putin's inner circle of oligarchs... with an intent of breaking the *okruzheniya* and shaking up the *siloviki* (a Praetorian guard that surrounded Putin and his inner circle)." In other words, start taking apart a traditional Russian nesting doll, a *matryoshka*, from the inside out.

Navalny sat in his cluttered office, 30 square meters—320 square feet—on the third floor for $530 a month. Located at 21 New Arbat Street. Easy walk to the Smolenskaya metro station. Shitty neighborhood, but he couldn't afford to squander funds. Piss-poor view of the towers in downtown Moscow, just enough space for his assistant, a couple of tables for volunteers, and a few cheap plastic chairs that could be used to host guests seated in front of his desk. Reeked of cigarettes and unwashed bodies.

Sent a single line of text to Fedor. "Visit."

Their signal, this month, that Navalny needed to speak with the computer whiz. Changed every thirty days. As did the location of their meetings. This month it was a place called "Coffee House." Typically, full of Generation Z types. Better than standing on a sidewalk. That *would* draw attention.

Not a bad stroll from his office and relatively convenient for Fedor. Navalny told his assistant he'd be back after running a few errands. Even she didn't know about his ties to Fedor.

August is a good time to wander the streets of Moscow. Freed of their Soviet-imposed work schedules, many Russians followed the European tradition of taking a holiday during that last month of summer. To the dacha, no matter how small, if they could afford one, or to the beaches of Crimea.

No one in Moscow cursed Putin's seizure of Crimea back in 2014. The Russian leader's continued pressure on Kiev ensured the Ukraine kept electricity flowing to the peninsula and, besides, the Americans were too tied up with the new Islamic caliphate to worry about events in central Europe. Regardless, the Black Sea was warm this time of year, sun was out, led to a rush of pasty-white chubby bodies headed for the shoreline.

Navalny had never been to Crimea. Not his idea of a vacation. His family owned a thousand-square-foot dacha thirty miles north of Moscow. Tucked away in the woods, the cabin was heated by a potbelly stove and suffered frequent electric outages. But it was an escape from the city. They would pile in, parents and his brother's wife and children. Played a lot of cards and drank copious quantities of vodka. Perfect holiday.

He knew IRI was suggesting he commit to the equivalent of killing Rasputin. Grigori Rasputin, the mad monk who promised Tsar Nicholas II and his bride that he could cure their son, Alexei, of hemophilia. One of those downsides of royal inbreeding, the heir-apparent suffered from a genetic defect that curtailed blood clotting. A minor cut or bruise could spell death. The 6-foot-4-inch-tall bearded religious man—many accused of being a charlatan—essentially took over the Russian government in cahoots with the tsar's wife when Nicholas II went to the western front in 1915. Pissed off the other

Russian elites, who conspired to rid themselves of the man. On the eve of 30 December 1916, he was invited to the home of Prince Felix Yusupov. Thereupon he was provided cyanide-laced cakes, which he ate with no apparent effect. Offered cyanide-laced wine and had three glasses, again to no apparent effect. Then shot three times. Thinking they were done with him, the plotters dumped his body in the Malaya Nevka River. Rumor has it that an autopsy found Rasputin finally died of drowning.

Navalny wondered if his IRI contacts knew that story. The nobles in question at the time were also engaged in a plot to dismantle a *matryoshka*, from the inside out. To no success. The monarchy in Russia only came to an end in 1917, when Tsar Nicholas II abdicated, a broken man.

Putin was unlikely to follow suit. Russians were not being slaughtered in a war, the economy had rebounded, and—aside from Navalny—there was no viable competition for assuming Putin's Kremlin apartments. And the unproclaimed new tsar's security detail had made it abundantly clear that Navalny was on a short leash. He walked with a permanent limp and fingernails were still missing on three of his ten digits.

And, yet, there he was, inside the Coffee House waiting to meet with Fedor.

Perhaps this explained why he had not given up over all these years. Unlike the stereotypical Russian, Navalny was an eternal optimist. Would probably get him killed one day—that was closer to normal Russian thinking—but, for the moment, he remained convinced that he, and he alone, could replace the aging KGB agent atop Moscow's political hierarchy.

Fedor was late, as usual. Rumpled and uncombed hair, as usual. Fit right in with a majority of the men wandering on New Arbat Street. Apart from the wealthy, Russian men were not going to win any fashion shows—he'd heard the same was true of men in Seattle, USA, but had never been there to make a comparison.

Fedor Ivanov was in no hurry. From long experience he knew it would take Navalny a bit of chat time before they got down to business. Then things would get serious. He fully expected to spend the next ninety minutes in Coffee House... an hour and a half absent from his opportunity to make money. Endless Horizons was humming; he'd just found a cheap supplier of Ecstasy. Shit sold like candy to the "club set" in Eastern Europe. This meeting was expensive—an observation he would not share with Navalny.

"What's up?" They'd settled down at a table in the very rear of the café.

"Suggestion from the Americans for ridding ourselves of a common friend." They never used Putin's name in electronic or even verbal conversation anywhere but at Navalny's dacha.

He then walked Fedor through the IRI email. An exchange of ideas completed through an electronic hub that included an encryption program designed to evaporate bits and bytes as soon as they were read—or before—if the wrong user accessed an account. There was no print option.

Fedor nodded. Muttered an affirmative response to the comments. Made no judgmental statements.

Simply offered the comment: "Blockchain."

Navalny gave him a blank stare.

"The foundation for Bitcoin."

More blank stares.

"Blockchain takes away dependence on a single server. Transactions are on a 'distributed ledger.' Fancy way of saying there are potentially thousands of machines recording each earning or expenditure. To hack into one solves nothing. You have to go past the 51 percent mark in order to create disorder and distrust."

He carried on.

"By the way, all those transactions are recorded and stored in what we call a hash tree. Means you can trace a Bitcoin from the day it was mined through all following owners to the present location. All of which is verifiable."

Fedor paused. This was going over Navalny's head. Too fucking bad, he needed to understand what they were about to accomplish.

"Bitcoin only survived this long because Satoshi Nakamoto—whoever he, she or it, might have been—back in 2008 figured out that in a system where mass collaboration exists, uncertainty is minimized. Fucking bankers never let you into their secrets, and with a blockchain there are potentially *no* secrets—unless you disguise your identity."

"And now you want to break in?" Fedor huffed. "And steal from Bitcoin wallets—the digital storage sites of the oligarch wealth ... good fucking luck. I'm not that smart."

Surprising modesty. A thought Navalny kept to himself.

"But," Fedor added, "I may know who is. We leave to make this call, then you can find a rental car from a cheap agency and contact me."

Navalny gave him a strange look.

"A cheap rental car won't be bugged. Your home, office, and vehicle probably are. Get it?"

"I'll pick you up in an hour." Navalny knew exactly the right place. Would take a metro ride to get there. They'd be traveling in the shittiest rental available in Moscow. "You sure all this is necessary?" The attorney in him coming out.

"You want to stay alive?" Fedor did not smile.

Which was how Dr. Bakshi found herself back on the phone with Fedor.

chapter 6

waiting for the other shoe to drop

moscow, russia, 20 august 2025

Adya Bakshi and Fedor Ivanov were "digital natives." Grew up in a world where computers always existed—they could not recall a time when the internet wasn't a daily feature—dictating everything from social contacts to educational opportunities. For "digital natives" the phrase "I'll Google it," was the 1950s equivalent of "look it up in the dictionary." Unfortunately, they both worked for "digital immigrants," the aged who could recall when the IBM Selectric typewriter was "state of the art." Some of those old farts still knew how to use a rotary phone and believed that faxing was high-speed communication.

Navalny should have been a "digital native," but had condemned himself to the "immigrant" status by going to law school. Budding attorneys in Russia were taught to handwrite on yellow legal pads; they typed on standalone computers running WordPerfect. Not because they were ignoring modernity, it was a bid to protect client privacy. The internet in Russia was presumed to be as insecure as the phone services. Particularly if you were in the business of defending individuals with objectives contradictory to Putin's agenda.

In other words, Navalny would nod north and south when Fedor started talking about encryption, the dark web, coding, and bits or bytes. He actually had no clue what the computer geek was describing, it was all just fucking magic to him.

Nonetheless, he took to heart Fedor's admonition concerning a safe locale for a phone call of a sensitive nature. Nothing better than a beat-up rental car. Would not draw law enforcement attention and was easy enough to sweep for listening devices—aka "bugs." That skill they did teach in Russian law schools. A minor detail he once let slip at an international legal conference. The Chinese and Pakistani attorneys all just nodded in a knowing manner, the Americans and Western European participants in that conversation were appalled.

He picked up Fedor at the Bulat Okudzhava Memorial at the corner of Arbat Street and Plotnikov Lane. An interesting choice. Okudzhava was a poet, musician, novelist, and song writer. Never overtly political, but always suspect back in the days when Russia was the Soviet Union. Navalny had a couple of Okudzhava's albums and admired his works. These days he was considered a bit of a folk hero—Russia's Bob Dylan. Best known for his poem and subsequent song: "Paper Soldier."

Once there lived a soldier-boy,
quite brave, one can't be braver,
but he was merely a toy
for he was made of paper.

He wished to alter everything,
and be the whole world's helper,
but he was a puppet on a string,
a soldier made of paper.

He'd bravely go through fire and smoke,
he'd die for you. No vapor.
But he was just a laughing-stock,
a soldier made of paper.

You would mistrust him and deny
your secrets and your favor.
Why should you do it, really, why?
'cause he was made of paper.

He dreads the fire? Not at all!
One day he cut a caper
and died for nothing; after all,
he was a piece of paper.

Navalny had no intention of becoming a paper soldier. He turned off Arbat Street onto Plotnikov Lane, then pulled curbside at the end of the memorial featuring a cast bronze table and benches. Fedor appeared within minutes. Still rumpled, and now sweaty from tromping over multiple blocks of the Arbat District.

"Bastard," he wheezed upon squeezing into the passenger seat. "Why did you forget to tell me a telephone store is more than a kilometer from your office?"

"You didn't ask." Navalny's lame response.

"Did you really think I was going to make this call on my phone? What the fuck did they teach you in law school?" Fedor was obviously peeved with the requirement to walk. The man reeked of cigarettes. Probably took out his anger on half a pack of the damn things during his adventure about the neighborhood.

For a moment, Navalny said nothing. Waited for his computer whiz to calm down and regain his breath. Then a simple question: "Where to?"

"Pick any back street near Gorky Park. Somewhere by the University of Design and Technology. Students drive crappy cars like this and park anywhere they can fit in. We won't draw attention that way—it's only twenty minutes from here, I'll have you back to work in an hour."

The car's air-conditioning didn't work. Fedor kept sweating.

They took back streets until they were able to access Smolenskiy Boulevard, crossed the Moskva River, and drove into the university's neighborhood. As promised, there was a collection of ratty cars jammed in haphazardly along the curbs. Fedor demanded they find a spot in the shade.

Once Navalny found a spot, Fedor pulled out his most recent

purchase—a burner. Cheap telephone with prepaid minutes purchased on a credit card he'd lifted from the web only twenty minutes before entering the shop. No questions asked during the entire exchange. Fedor knew what he was purchasing, the store owner knew he'd clear the transaction before the phone left his location. Had been through this type of transaction a thousand times before. Really did not have any interest in what this phone was going to be used for. Just assumed it was not legal. Welcome to Moscow.

Fedor made his call. Had memorized her new number. He wanted no slips of paper in the event something went wrong. Fucking Moscow police and Putin's security patrols were a random threat that could materialize any moment. He'd actually eaten notes scribbled on a page during one unfortunate surprise visit from the cops.

Bakshi answered on the third ring, despite the fact it was 0425 in Montgomery. Like Fedor, she tended to work at night and sleep during the day, another vampire.

"Time we talk, doctor." Fedor skipped introductions. "You recall our deal, yes?"

She didn't hesitate. "Yes."

"You are going to help me with an issue involving cryptocurrency, Bitcoin to be exact. Understand? We want into the blockchain, or more accurately, we want into the blockchain for a select group of individuals. I will pass information to you in an encrypted email. Are you still listening?"

"Yes." Much more unease in her voice, tangible even through the cheap device Fedor was using.

"When do you need this done by?"

A question Fedor had forgotten to ask Navalny. He turned to the politician. "How soon?"

"Election is set for March, next year. But we want to send the Kremlin into chaos months before. Say, 1 November."

A deadline that gave the good doctor less than seventy days to take the names Fedor was to send, discover their identities within the blockchain, seize control of the trail for their hash-marked accounts, divert funds to another location on the internet—and pull it all off undetected.

Fedor just stared at Navalny. Gave him that look of "do you know how fucking hard this is going to be?" And then passed the date to Bakshi.

"Okay." She was almost whispering now. "When can I expect the names?"

"In the next three hours." Fedor was giving himself a lot of time to get back to his apartment. He'd done enough exercise today. The next step in this adventure would require a stop for beer and more cigarettes.

"I'll watch for the 'package.'" Her final comment. And then the phone went dead.

Fedor climbed out from the car. Stood on the curb and first pulled the flash memory card—a feature common to most burners—then dropped the phone on the pavement and ground it beneath his heel into a collection of plastic bits and pieces. Final disposition of the mess was to push the lot, including the flash memory, into a curbside storm sewer grate.

Time for step two in this game.

"Drop me off at the Arabatskaya metro station. I need to get home. You need to get rid of this car."

No comment from Navalny, he just put the vehicle into gear and joined the rest of Moscow's notorious traffic.

Dr. Bakshi put down her phone and took a deep breath. Then typed a short email to her business partners: "Meet for lunch tomorrow... Dreamland BBQ." She was no fan of American barbecue, but figured bad news was best delivered over a meal the boys favored. Plus, it was a short walk to the Montgomery Riverwalk Stadium. She wasn't much for baseball, but the minor league Biscuits' games reminded her of cricket, and the stadium sat only seven thousand, so there was no sense of being overwhelmed by a crowd. Wouldn't hurt to sweeten the pot with a set of tickets for that afternoon's game. Made the reservations for a three-pack of "super box seats"—for a grand sum of fifty dollars—and then logged off.

Rather than head for a shower and then bed, the usual end of her day, she grabbed a notepad and pen. Drew three lines down the length of the first page, creating separate columns with the titles: "Vulnerabilities," "Access," and "Consequences." Would normally have done this sorting on an Excel spreadsheet, but was taking zero chances with Fedor. He could hack her phone and probably gain access to her laptop, but he couldn't steal paper electronically, unless she left it in sight of a camera. Thinking of which, she reached up with a piece of painter's tape and covered the laptop's camera. Did the same to her iPhone.

One risk down. Countless more to consider.

She went back to her columns. Began with "Vulnerabilities."

There were obvious starting points:

1. Users—always target the weakest link... humans.

2. Authentication—proof of identification... with blockchain software the users create a "seed phrase" of twelve words that are then transformed via software into a string of sixty-four patternless characters known as a "private key." There is no way to reverse the "private key" back to the twelve words... which meant she was reconsidering vulnerability number 1, users.

3. Authorization—this came with three options:

    a. Something you know—typically a password... that would be option number two, authentication.

    b. Something you have—a physical component like an ATM card.

c. Something physical—biometrics... laptops and phones had long ago gone to facial recognition or fingerprints. Retinal scanning went out with the 1990s, too expensive, and DNA recognition was reserved for the most extreme cases... i.e., access to NSA's bank of super computers.

4. Computing requirements—users did not only need to be able to authenticate so the software could authorize, for Bitcoin they required a ridiculous amount of electricity. Little known to most Americans, Germans, or South Koreans, "mining" a new Bitcoin burned the equivalent of about the same amount of electricity an average American household would consume in two years. Yes, two years. Some analysts argued the energy necessary to maintain the Bitcoin network over a twenty-four-hour period was the equivalent of that used by many medium-sized nations.

This last vulnerability was a sore point among Bitcoin "miners" and environmentalists.

When Bitcoin started back in 2008 it was possible to mine for "coins" at home using a laptop. Then, to keep the cryptocurrency valuable, the math algorithm one had to solve became increasingly complicated—requiring an increasing amount of computing power to generate a single "coin." You ate electricity to power and cool the chain of machines a power user would set up in their house or small commercial building. Reached the point where the "superusers" could be identified by the amount of juice they burned in comparison to what a producer of physical goods consumed.

Enraged environmentalists used that data to hunt down and identify the superusers. There was a site online and occasional newspaper story that named the culprits.

Bad for them, good for her.

A super-user was likely to have all the ledgers necessary to track down specific Bitcoin giants. And shutting down enough super-users might serve to give her access to the blockchain.

Which brought her to the final vulnerability.

5. Blockchain software—with the increasing popularity of Bitcoin and other cryptocurrencies, blockchain programs were readily available. Just like Microsoft or Apple coding, there were likely backdoors in the blockchain system. Crack into the software that drove this whole fiasco and she could "pwn" (old hacker joke) the entire charade.

(The original word was "pwned"... typed in by a hacker who exercised poor keyboard skills, so when he went to gloat about his latest accomplishments the email was full of misspellings. The word should have been "owned." "Pwned" became the phrase of choice for computer geeks who would seize control of someone's system or network.)

This applied to Bitcoin via the "51 percent attack" rule. If someone could control more than 50 percent of the computing power used for mining, they could write an alternative financial history via blockchain.

This meant funds could be stolen and moved to other accounts without leaving a trace.

Obviously, vulnerability 5 would be the ultimate objective. And the most difficult to achieve. Getting administrator or "root access" to blockchain was the holy grail of hacking.

Column two—"Access"—was in some ways simpler, and in others, more difficult than vulnerabilities.

1. Users—only in this case she was considering all options. The mantra of cyber security gurus is: "confidentiality, integrity, availability." Confidentiality meant keeping data—like passwords—private. Integrity translated to preventing unauthorized tampering with the system or data there within. Availability was ensuring users could use the system when they desired. She bet the fastest route was cracking confidentiality—hence the focus on users.

2. World Wide Web—Bitcoin lived and died on the internet. Which meant data passed through no small number of servers—router software was notoriously ridden with backdoors and zero-day defects. Was a matter of finding one that would provide her anonymous access to the blockchain collective. Time to do some homework on Huawei routers—the cheapest—and thus most popular choice for service providers.

3. Thousands of dedicated computers—given Bitcoin's popularity, the number of machines dedicated to mining and maintaining the blockchain was somewhat unimaginable. Opening the door to gaining access via a botnet—malware that took over a person's computer for a use other than what they intended—often without ever garnering attention from the owner. She could code with the best of them. The trick was planting a bot. Spear phishing, using an attachment in an official-looking email to launch a program once the user clicked on a supposedly secure document, was such an old trick it rarely functioned as a ploy these days. But never underestimate that human propensity to make foolish mistakes. Write the right botnet and it would take only one user to unleash the demon that undid them all.

She was running out of mental energy. Column three—"Consequences."

1. Success—deliver the data Fedor was demanding and he would set her free. Unlikely he'd be so beneficent. That undesirable consequence could go further down on the list.

2. Obtain access to significant wealth—if she pulled this off there was no reason Bakshi could not also load her own account with misbegotten funds. Given her present occupation, she was already no paragon of virtue. Why not ensure a future retirement and take care of the parents?

3. Reputation—this was a dual-edged sword. If she succeeded and word leaked out, well, here was an opportunity to be known as the hack who accomplished what no one else had been able to do. On the other hand, if she succeeded and word leaked out there was also the possibility of reciprocal attacks, and this frightened her. She was aware of the fact Putin set loose men to sever the hands of hackers he held responsible for attacks on his administration. If nothing else, there was the possibility of prison. Washington had also grown weary of the hacking community, and proved more than willing to prosecute.

4. Endless tasking—back to Fedor—and the issue of reputation. If she pulled this off Fedor could blackmail her into repeat performances. She would never be free of the Russian bastard. And, given the rapidity with which he'd found her, then he likely would be able to locate her parents.

5. Second and third effects—this was a consequence that could play out in either a positive or negative manner... or both.

Dr. Bakshi pushed aside the paper and dropped her pen on the table. The clock flashed 0530. Time to sleep if she was going to meet the boys for lunch. Figuring she would shower after crashing as a means of waking up, Bakshi crawled under the covers still in her street clothes. Set the alarm for 1100 and drifted off into a restless slumber.

Didn't bother to check her email for a message from Fedor. That could wait another five hours.

Back in Moscow, Navalny was now just three blocks from the car rental lot. At block three he'd taken a hard right turn onto a side street and pulled into a parking garage he knew. Drove to the top deck, where he sat in the afternoon sun. Still warm, but empty up here.

Muscovites don't like the heat, and sure as shit do not want to climb five flights to a car that's been baking all day.

He fished though his sports jacket pocket and extracted a burner that looked almost the same as the phone Fedor had dumped into the sewer ninety minutes ago. The computer whiz was not the only one who knew to purchase throwaways when making sensitive calls.

He had to admit, however, Fedor was on the mark about getting the car. Significantly diminished the chance of purposeful or accidental collection of his next telephone conversation.

Dialed a number he'd been instructed to memorize and never, ever write down or save on a communications device of any kind.

Two rings, then, "Hello?" Always the same answer, regardless of what time of night or day he called. In clear American English.

"Checking in."

"Go ahead." The unidentified voice response.

"Boy Wonder has set loose the hounds."

"Where are the dogs?"

Navalny thought for a moment. "I don't know. But the prefix was 8-10-1-334. I did not catch the rest. The person who answered was definitely a woman. Sounded like she was from India or Pakistan."

"That's helpful." No further comment.

"I will call if or when there is more information." With that Navalny hung up.

At headquarters in Langley the faceless phone monitor set his receiver back onto its cradle. Then jotted notes into an email that was sent immediately to the team working Russian human operations. The email title: "Time to call the veterinarian."

In Washington, DC, it was 0700 on 26 August 2025—a Tuesday. The key players were already checking their electronic in-boxes.

chapter 7

running with the big dogs
washington, dc, 22 august 2025

I don't care how big your crisis is, don't fuck with my gym time. A woman has to take care of herself—not an easy task when you're stuck in a wheelchair. Nice thing about living on Capitol Hill: Results—the gym. Place used to be an abandoned schoolhouse parked right upside the I-395 viaduct. Turns out the historical preservation types wouldn't allow it to be torn down, so it went through a massive interior renovation. Now features three floors of means to torture yourself.

That's where my morning starts, at 0600, seven days a week. I lift weights, do aerobics, and take a variety of classes, including yoga and a self-defense course tailored for us "handicapped" folks. Spent about ninety minutes each visit to Results. Was in the best shape of my life. Never brought the phone with me. Too damn tempting to answer a call or check email. Learned that lesson during the first week of starting there.

Took a shower—they'd totally fitted the place out for us special-needs types—and made it back home by 0810. Poured a cup of coffee and toasted a bagel—the "everything" variety. I like food with flavor.

Then, and only then, did I sit down to the computer. I'm set up for facial recognition to access the machine that gets all my communications. The boxes that take care of other business have a dual verification system. Facial recognition and a random number entry requirement. That random number is generated every five minutes and distributed to users via a secured microwave broadcast that appears on a plastic device about the size of USB stick. So, I smile at the machine's camera and then punch in the current nine-digit code.

Nothing's perfect, but it would protect my data if someone broke into the house. That and my Doberman. Wiper has no sense of humor. Named him after a virus that took out a mountain of hard drives at the Iranian Oil Ministry back in 2012. Couple him with the best home security system you can purchase—including all windows replaced with shatterproof glass. No one is fucking with my shit.

Pulled up my unclassified email account for the Agency. Typical collection of administrative notices and items passed along by colleagues who are either being helpful or looking for help—usually more of the latter than the former. Nature of my job: Try to solve problems at home while breaking dishes abroad.

Oh, here's a trick I learned a couple of years ago. Rather than reading my email from the most current to the oldest, I tackle my in-box in reverse. Took to heart a comment some management consultant offered during CIA mandatory training classes: "Keep an empty email in-box." She suggested building a set of folders to store items that served reference purposes, but insisted that "if you start each day by looking at the problems you didn't address yesterday they will get appropriate attention—not lost in the ether."

That meant it took me about thirty minutes to hit "Time to call the Veterinarian."

Still can tell you when I opened the email... 0851. Was about ten minutes ahead of my "normal" report-in schedule of 0900. (Another thing that management consultant taught me: "Train your boss to expect a set work appearance schedule, or you will be on the hook 24/7.") There was nothing I could do about the hours clocked after

I reported in, but that 0900 thing kept my gym routine safe from the front-office taskmasters.

"Shit." My first reaction.

As expected, there was no content in the email, just that subject line: "Time to call the Veterinarian."

Here's the issue—*I'm* "the Veterinarian."

Ops team came up with that title after we ran into the market crash in 2022 and Merkel's bitter failure to win another term atop the German political hierarchy—both events attributed to Russian cyber warfare. CIA was specifically directed—via the Oval Office—to prevent any further such debacles. The CIA director was handed control of CYBERCOM. White House took it away from the NSA director, who had always been dual-hatted since they first stood up the military's computer war machine. Brutal politics—at least at the bureaucratic level in the intelligence community. Pretty much rendered the director of National Intelligence a powerless position, a collection of pencil-pushers we'd ignored for years, despite the fact they worked out of a building only four miles up Highway 123.

After I led a team that shut down North Korea's efforts to again penetrate SWIFT and then helped design software that nuked Pyongyang's internet servers, my reputation was made—even on the Ops side of the Agency.

Was told to be at my first meeting in the Ops secured conference room over eighteen months ago. They went through the usual mumbo jumbo of "reading me in" to a variety of operations and highly sensitive contacts in all our favorite cyber adversary nations. You know, China, India, Iran, Israel, North Korea, South Korea . . . and, of course, Russia. Then started providing me with a list of names that would be an indication of a potential disaster in the making.

Failed to mention many of those names were also on the CIA payroll—a collection of traitors who were giving us the goods.

Sometimes.

You never know when a foreign operative is now working on an agenda quite different from what Washington desires.

Also divulged a list of what were considered the most dangerous hackers currently in business. Had obviously spent more than a bit of time working to link online call signs with real names. Managed to even purchase the loyalty of a few of the most notorious black-hat types. But there were a hell of a lot more names on that black-hat list who'd told the CIA to go to hell and were still wreaking havoc.

Funny thing about the Russian list, I still distinctly recall these eighteen months later: Putin, who was, obviously, at the top, immediately followed by his most famous opponent, Alexei Navalny. After that, identities were for all the usual suspects, you know, head of intelligence, heads of commercial, official . . . and unofficial . . . computer centers, a few known bad actors, and a plethora of suspected ring leaders in the Russian hacking community.

Anyway, I was informed that I was to be the lead for efforts at warding off strategic-level problems in the cyberworld when it came to handling attempts to manipulate information or hack into critical functions. Specifically, aircraft control systems, banking, Wall Street market exchanges, and heads of state. Was also told to ignore denial of service silliness and hacking to steal identities or credit cards. "The small stuff" was how the Ops chief put it. "Leave that for CYBERCOM and the kids downstairs here."

"Why 'the Veterinarian'?" My first question after being told this was to be my call sign.

"You're responsible for rounding up and curing the big dogs." Reasonable answer, or so I thought. At least it wasn't "Sewer Rat" or "Computer Queen." I'd bet money the bastards in Ops had considered those options. It's their kind of warped humor.

Back to the present.

Picked up my encrypted cell phone and dialed the same workspace Navalny had called only two hours ago. "This is the Veterinarian, when is the first meeting?"

Short pause. "Sixty minutes from now, in the Ops conference room."

Click.

Damn good thing I own that Tesla Model X. At least the worst of rush hour was over. By now the George Washington Parkway from Spout Run to the Agency's back gate would be a high-speed transit route. Any cop in pursuit of my vehicle would be stopped by CIA security at the gate and told to forget the whole event. Those guys with hats and guns who keep the Agency safe all knew when it was time to push back on local law enforcement. Didn't hurt they had access to a database listing names and license plate numbers for employees who might require a little assistance with the traffic law enforcement kids.

Wheeled out the door at 0910. Had a reserved handicapped sign installed on the curb in front of the house, so the Tesla was always available. Learned to park facing the wrong direction, so accessing the driver's side door was easy. Hoisted myself in, reached around and did a quick collapse to flat with my chair, and tossed it through the rear passenger gull-wing door into an empty space that used to be a back seat. Told you, I stay in shape.

Can't speed through the neighborhood. Too many nannies, children, and citizens who know me. I wouldn't get a ticket, but the snake-eye from locals during my Saturday morning trips to Eastern Market would make for an uncomfortable breakfast and shopping excursion.

Caught the I-395 viaduct at the 7th Street on-ramp.

Relatively speaking, 395 was empty. When I bought this vehicle I had them move the accelerator and brakes to paddles on the steering wheel column. You know, just like the shifters for those overpriced Lexus toys. Set it up like a motorcycle—accelerator paddle on the right, brake paddle on the left. I was right at home.

Whipped through the remnants of rush hour and hit the GW Parkway. Kept within the speed limit until I passed the exit for

Roosevelt Island parking, then let the Model X go. Nothing like running the Parkway on a gorgeous August morning at 110 mph.

Made the back gate at CIA in under seventeen minutes.

They don't check badges anymore, just use biometric scanning gear that reads through glass. Was immediately waved through. Helped to know the guards—they recognized the Tesla. Not too many black women driving one of these things into CIA HQ.

The Agency has a parking design that provides for lot and street parking all the way around the two buildings that constitute headquarters. Have to do that when you own a campus with 2.5 million square feet of office space and god knows how many employees on-site at any given time. This is when it *helps* to be handicapped. I have reserved parking at the northeast entrance. Puts me in at ground level—a quick roll to the Ops conference room. Unlike the Analyst side, Ops likes to stay out of sight, plus the space was available. No one else wanted a windowless tomb for meetings.

Place was half-full when I arrived at 0950.

PowerPoint slides were ready for projection—the standard intro cover slide was already displayed on a screen in the front of the room.

Doors closed at 1000, sharp. Ops director didn't brook tardy meeting attendees. Man stood all of five feet eight inches. Kept in shape, but was now bald and as nearsighted as a bat. White guy. Did you expect a "brother" in that position? Get over yourself. For an older white boy he did his best to keep up with his field personnel. Obviously ran the miles and hit a weight room a couple of times a week.

He looked around the room—I'd already done the same—some I recognized, others were obviously fresh college graduates. The world changes in eighteen months. None of these people would be present if they hadn't been "read in" to this program. And no one except the security personnel and the Ops director and his deputy were kept informed as to who was in or out of a particular operation. Kept people—all of whom should have known better—from chitchatting in the hallways or at lunch.

Opening remarks were short. "You all should know why you are here, at least at the macro level. Now we add some detail. This morning at 0650 Alexei Navalny called in. Offered a single warning, 'Boy Wonder has set loose the hounds.' Navalny had no identification for the 'hounds' except a set of telephone prefixes that led to a number registered in Montgomery, Alabama. Said the person on the other side was female and likely from India or Pakistan. That's it."

Thought he was done, but he wasn't.

"Here's the kicker, 'Wonder Boy' is the call sign for Fedor Ivanov that we agreed Navalny would use in such a situation." He looked around. "A few of you have more background on Fedor?"

Fucking Ops and cyber types, no one wants to share data; keep the *glory* to yourself. Exactly why the Oval Office had assigned CYBERCOM to CIA. Now we were back to the bad old ways.

I put an end to this crap.

"Fedor is arguably one of the best in the world. Been in and out of more secured systems than most of us can name. That includes all major telephone data bases, SWIFT, and the source coding for ArcSight—that's HP shit, for you who don't know—SAP, Symantec, and McAfee. In other words, he knows where the holes are in most of the security programs run on government, industry, and private machines.

"He's also developed an expertise in dark web marketing, runs a site called Endless Horizons. You can purchase almost anything you desire. Just a warning, once you log in, he has access to everything on the machine used to contact Endless Horizons. The name is appropriate—you get what you want, he gains access to yet another machine and all associated data and email contacts saved there on. Been known to use Conficker-style attacks to create botnets, then wait to launch upon his command—frequently, denial of service attacks—without the owner ever knowing the malware was resident on their now 'dormant zombie' laptop. We think he may have as many as two million zombies just waiting to be awakened."

A hand shot up. "Before you go any further, explain 'botnet' in plain English. We're not all computer geeks here."

I looked at the Ops director—pissed at this interruption—but he indicated I should answer the question.

"I'll kill two birds with one stone. Conficker first appeared in 2008. It took advantage of a zero-day vulnerability in Microsoft Windows to access a computer, disguise itself under a random file name in the root directory, and then build a botnet. Some experts like to consider Conficker a worm—a worm that built the largest botnet ever—over seven million computers were infected with the software. Problem is, no one ever figured out what the botnet was supposed to do or who wrote the software. As for the name—likely a mashup of an old domain name, trafficconverter.biz, or a play on the German word for 'fucker.' That's your trivial pursuit for the day. As for a botnet. In plain English, a botnet is a network of machines that have been covertly or, occasionally, overtly, hijacked, loaded with some bit of nefarious software—what most of you would call malware—and then set into action. Some botnets are used to steal information, that's what we think Conficker was supposed to do. Others exist to shut down a targeted system or systems—what you commonly hear called a distributed denial of service—DDOS."

I let all that sink in for a second.

"The beauty of botnets, there is no geographic limit on from where they are constructed, launched, or what target they are after, so long as enough of the infected machines have access to the internet. Also, the owner of the zombie machine typically has no idea he or she is contributing to the malicious activity. And, best of all, even when we detect the malicious activity, forensic analysis usually only allows for identification of a machine or machines conducting the attack—we almost never discover who crafted the original worm or where they are operating from. To this day, we don't know who put Conficker into play. With me now?"

Heads in the room nodded north and south. The Ops director gave me a nod. "Continue."

I did.

"Here's what worries me about this phone call. Fedor never leaves Russia, and never works with anyone else. He's written his own firewall and security software that keep his machines away from prying eyes—including mine, and not for lack of trying, believe me. I know why he never leaves Russia—he's afraid of Interpol and any other national law enforcement entity that would provide for his extradition to the United States. Most of the Russian hackers realize their days of foreign travel are long over, so Fedor's decision on that front comes as no surprise."

I was in free-flow mode now.

"But what's more worrisome is this decision to apparently reach out for assistance or an accomplice. If he's doing that he's after one of the internet's holy grails. The question is which one? It'd be a big job and he's probably on a tight schedule. Or, worse yet, it's a combination of the two ... Now, I have a question for someone on the analysis side. What's Fedor doing with Navalny? Never saw anything on the web indicting Fedor was into politics."

A hand in the back of the room went up, slowly. A mousy older guy with thick glasses and a bad Russian accent. "Fedor wasn't, his father was. Worked internal investigations at SVR. Was killed for getting too close to Putin's allies with incriminating information."

"You know this how?" I guess my incredulity came across a little too obviously.

"I worked SVR internal investigations as well. I fled Russia when Fedor's father was killed. You might say I was his partner."

That one shut me down for a moment. Forgot the Agency hired former adversaries and then gave them top clearances.

"OK, so Fedor'sworking for Navalny now?"

The old analyst again. "Yes, that is what I would assume. Navalny is not so crazy as to go searching for a hacker; he must know such an act would cause unrest in the Kremlin."

"Which means Fedor is looking to create a problem for Putin?"

"Russian presidential elections are scheduled for March 2026," my font of wisdom from the backroom replied. "Putin has no identified successor and is likely to decide he will hold onto office by manipulating the constitution, electorate, and, ultimately, the ballots themselves. Again. Navalny probably sees his one chance to end this ambition by starting to derail Putin now."

"It would obviously take time." My observation. Needed to make him walk through the entire argument, which he did.

"Navalny will have to recruit press attention, draw in other politicians, and convince a majority of Russians it is time for Putin to go. No easy job—requires what the Chinese would call 'unrestricted warfare'—economic, information, legal, and, perhaps, even physical attacks. He would also need to break Putin's *okruzheniya,* the inner circle of oligarchs who have every reason—billions of them in some cases—to keep the new tsar in power."

"That would explain Navalny contacting Fedor, but why then reach out to us?"

"Perhaps, Navalny thinks Fedor and whoever he called in the U.S. are not enough to counter the Kremlin. Perhaps. Or, Navalny is looking to play the cyber world against itself while he takes a different approach ... what you Americans call 'create a distraction.'"

The analyst took a deep breath, obviously a longtime smoker.

"There is one more consideration—we are talking Russian politics, where there is a plot, within a plot, within a plot. I have frequently wondered why Navalny is not in prison or dead. He escapes where all others fail. Even when he goes to jail Navalny is almost immediately back on the street and does not appear to have been too badly beaten, by Russian standards. That requires protection from someone very well-placed in the Kremlin."

Shit, now my head was spinning. Was I being asked to stop Fedor or help him? Were we going to be caught in a trap that would divulge our own carefully honed and tightly protected capabilities—either via Fedor or his new partner? And *was* it a partner, or just a hired hand with some new code?

Too many questions. Too few answers.

chapter 8

rolling through lightning looking for a leash

washington, dc, 25 august 2025

Who let the prophet of doom in this room?

If the old bastard was right, we'd have no definitive indication of Navalny's intentions. In the counterintelligence world he would likely already be stacking up nominations as a classic double agent. You know, the guys who spy on their own nation, turn over the data, and then spy on your nation. Good gig if you can get it and stay alive—or, at the very least, out of jail. Imagine, paid by both employers and repeatedly congratulated for the great work. Just need to decide where to retire—if you survive.

That's a big *if.* The downside to working in the ops world is an abject necessity to never trust anyone. Unless the breathing being in question is your dog, and even that can be a risky proposition.

Thinking of which, the Ops director was now looking at me in that manner one associates with more bad news coming.

"The Veterinarian has lead on this one. I expect full cooperation and an update brief from you—Roller—at least every seventy-six hours."

Shit, the man used my other call sign. At least he didn't out me as "Tiana," then some of these assholes could have looked me up on the web. There are no last names at CIA, except in the classified email.

Or via a database stored only on the high-side system. That's the Intelink network.

Have I told you about this before? Intelink went live in 1994. Came out as three versions: Intelink-U (the unclassified stuff), Intelink-S (secret-level silliness), and Intelink-TS (where they hide all the material that only the spooks and a few policy makers get to read). Looks just like the internet—has most of the same search engines and software, just gives a "cleared" person access to most of the crap produced by the kids who do HUMINT, IMINT, MASINT and SIGINT.

Goddamn it, now I have to explain all the IC lingo.

Like all good bureaucrats and the military, we have our own set of shortcuts. Who wants to spell out Human Intelligence, when HUMINT will do? Same with the other "ints"—all of them should be obvious—IMINT is imagery intelligence, SIGINT is signals intelligence. The only mystery is MASINT: measures and signals intelligence.

Here's the tricky part: who collects it and what the title really means. I'm going to start with HUMINT. Human intelligence is the old-fashioned business of extracting information from other people, preferably ones who have something of value to add to our understanding of an issue that is worrying policy makers. CIA and the Defense Intelligence Agency are both tasked with HUMINT missions. The CIA should be working political targets; the DIA is supposed to be focused on military concerns. In reality, the two agencies cross lanes every day of the week. As a result, they compete for sources and sometimes pay the same guy for the same information (that's called a "clever thief" in my world). Problem with HUMINT is that, unlike a reputable newspaper, the IC will run with a single source... hence the nightmare in Iraq with "Curveball."

How about IMINT. Imagery intelligence is primarily done by the National Geospatial-Intelligence Agency, also known as NGA. Should be NGIA, but a former director figured out three-letter agencies get more respect on Capitol Hill than four-letter agencies. So, he pulled a semantic fast one on the legislators, who apparently were not quick on the draw. Yeah, yeah, the NGA guys look at all the pictures—standard photos, including color (no more shades of gray), radar, and infrared—what we pull from outer space and some of the stuff culled from drones or other air-breathing assets like the U-2. Sexy shit, gives the senior decision-makers a hard-on. Drawback—you can fool photography. It's called denial and deception. Either the target hides the object of interest, or they make it look like something else.

Now we get to the fun one, MASINT. Launch a rocket for test purposes and we'll track its telemetry, heat signature, and flight profile. They really have rocket scientists looking at this shit. The primary collector is DIA, but everyone—particularly CIA's Weapons Intelligence Non-Proliferation and Arms Control Center (WINPAC)—likes to join the game. The WINPAC kids are real prima donnas. They actually believe they know everything, just ask them. Hate, hate, hate going to meetings with the WINPAC folks.

That brings me to SIGINT. Yeah, not hard to guess who does this; NSA—No Such Agency. To be honest we should break this down into separate categories, COMINT (communications intelligence), and SIGINT (signals intelligence). COMINT is exactly what you think it is, listening to other people's conversations, regardless of the language. That's why the military teaches a fair number of people to speak foreign tongues. But they also read intercepted messages from almost any source—paper, broadcast, and email. SIGINT, on the other hand, is all about the "noise" that radars and other similar systems make. The SIGINT kids can trace anything from aircraft to ships using their ability to "fingerprint" an electronic signal.

Oh, one more comment. The NSA folks like to refer to their shit as "SIGINT fact." Let me tell you, honey, COMINT is the same as HUMINT; gossip is gossip, even if you collect it via a hundred-million-dollar satellite.

Notice anything missing here?

Yup. *My* job.

The bureaucrats and academics have not yet managed to derive a sexy abbreviation for IC hackers. Shit, for a long time they refused to believe we were of any value—unless it was to steal data. Back in the 2015 timeframe, a full 90 percent of the hackers at CYBERCOM only worked defense, another 9 percent did "admin" work, and there was just a paltry 1 percent of us who worked offense. Made Congress and the intelligence leadership nervous... apparently afraid the offensive side at CYBERCOM or CIA (when they discovered my job existed) would be busy changing their messages and software. Idiots. The best defense is offense. They apparently didn't learn *that* tried-and-true lesson in high school. We came along and changed the game. Sure, CIA could go out and kill people, but they had no idea of how to screw up their lives on the internet first.

I did. Started out in a relatively simple manner. Turn off the connections. Frequently that was simply a matter of cutting a telephone wire, at least back in the good old days. Then it became a denial of service, morphed to fucking around with email accounts, and became really sophisticated when we arrived at manipulating Facebook pages and news stories online. Just ask Hillary Clinton about the 2016 election.

Got even better when someone figured out you could screw up business and political ambitions just by manipulating the number of "friends" or "followers" a target had on Facebook or Twitter. For a while the Agency had a slush fund tucked away by selling bots—computer generated identities—for about a penny apiece. The desperate political types would purchase "loyal" followers twenty-five thousand at a time. Just remember, what Caesar giveth, Caesar taketh away. One day you're popular, the next day you're not.

Well, baby, I can take away your bank account, sell your shares on Wall Street, and disown your children. Betting your wife will be pissed about the pictures of you and that twenty-something mistress I planted on your phone. And your boss is going to be real peeved about the "diverted" funds that seemingly fueled your new gambling addiction.

All done before you even wake up tomorrow. Told you I don't sleep much.

Still, I needed some more input from this collection of "wise heads." I took a look around the conference room and then asked that fatal question, "Someone want to volunteer ideas on where to start?"

Oh, a little more trivial pursuit about working with the government. When hands go up among those with experience dealing with "pols" (that would be "politicals" in our world) we've got shortcuts, just like the military. For instance, an insider refers to the president's workspace as the "Oval," not the "Oval Office." That's a term employed by amateurs. Same thing is true of the room where the Joint Chiefs of Staff meet—that's the "Tank." Hey, if you want to look and sound like a world-weary Beltway professional, you need to know the language.

Including hand signals.

When a question goes out for consumption in a Washington insiders' meeting, raising a hand with just the index finger pointing up means you have something substantive to add. If you pair that index finger with its accompanying digit, then you have a significant point and some minor crap to accompany the first observation—if the room has time for that follow-up silliness. Hey, you need to know this shit if you're going to survive among the untamed egos running amok in DC or northern Virginia.

First hand up with a single digit was a young man who couldn't wait to be called on. Just blurted out, "I presume you know Navalny is seeking to embarrass Putin. So we hack his email, out and freeze his bank accounts, and post some fake skin shots, the standard crap."

I just stared at the kid. Then I pulled a classic example of poor management.

"How long you been working this problem set?" This is a question loaded with judgment. It insinuates the target is still wet behind the ears and wasting everyone's time. I've been told over and over that millennials and Gen Z types get really upset with this approach. Well, fuck that, you don't get a trophy just for being here. You want a pat on the back for just showing up? Go see your parents. *My* folks demanded we provide something of value *before* we opened our mouths in public.

Still, this punk didn't take the clue. His smug answer, issued in a demeaning tone, was "Eighteen months."

Cue Angry Black Woman.

"Let me help you with this." I wasn't going to put up with his bullshit for however long we all had to work together. "I've been in this wheelchair five years now, and I still make mistakes concerning my capabilities. I've smacked my face on the floor more than once. You might want to consider that lesson." The kid went silent, looking lost and forsaken.

"We've been after Putin for more than two decades; the man doesn't use email. Has *no* personal financial records we've been able to find, and manipulates the press better than any occupant of the White House has ever managed to accomplish. But, I'm sure your *extensive* experience has *already* revealed those facts. Yes?"

Now the kid got it. I bet he stays quiet the rest of this year.

"Anyone else have an idea?"

That cough of phlegm was back. He held up two fingers.

"Yes, go ahead."

"You will not get Putin on the web. Navalny has to know that. His 'Fifth Season of the Year' foundation failed at trying just such a tactic after three years of foreign and domestic funding. All he succeeded in doing was pissing off Putin and putting young men and women in jail under the charge of treason. If, *if*, you want Putin you must go after the *okruzheniya*, his inner circle. They are all men who owe Putin their fortunes, and none of them trust him. They also don't trust each other. Putin survives because he could teach lessons to Machiavelli. This Navalny also knows."

He coughed and carried on, and I let him.

"If I was Navalny, I would go after the oligarchs. Take away that which they treasure most—money. I would be very surprised if any of the *okruzheniya* keep large accounts in Russian banks. Too easy for Putin or his *siloviki*—security personnel—to raid the funds. I would suggest Navalny is looking elsewhere. The internet. That would explain his relationship with Fedor Ivanov."

"Online banking?" My honest question.

"Online currency. And only one is completely trusted. Bitcoin."

Ops director raised an eyebrow at me; only hair left on his head.

And Soviet throwback gave me a questioning look, like I *don't* know about Bitcoin. Give me a fucking break. I'll say this, the old man was on his game. I hadn't made that connection. To be honest, I kept up with all things Russia only by reading the newspaper. And was way too damn poor to afford Bitcoin. At $35,000 a pop, the "coins" were well outside the price range of a federal employee. I still banked in the old-fashioned dollar bill.

"So," I said, "if Navalny is going after the oligarch wealth, how do we tell who the targets will be?" I'm milking the old man for all he's worth. The damn internet is huge, and I already know shopping through blockchain is no cake walk. Helped the FBI with an issue there a few years back. The suspect went free; we could never get his identification linked to income or expenditures. And that son of a bitch was selling people—people—like when my great-, great-, great-grandparents were shipped to this country. Only this scumbag was in the sex trade. Nobody buys servants or field hands anymore.

"The inner circle bickers among itself." Old guy again. "Make them suspicious of theft or traitors in the ranks and things will go badly. Fast. Navalny knows this as well. He has not survived so long without a number of bear hugs and three kisses."

I gave him a puzzled look.

"Traditional means of greeting a close acquaintance. You Americans think a handshake will do. Not in Russia."

"Where are the fractures? The personalities that will come to blows soonest? I presume that is what Navalny is looking to exploit." I was catching on to this analyst's game, at the same time I was hoping to carve down the search time spent on discovering Fedor and his sidekick's intentions.

"Good questions." The old man was now a center of attention in a room of self-proclaimed experts. "I will have to go back to my desk and do some digging. I believe my younger counterpart will be happy to help." A clear dig at the prick I'd shot down only minutes before. Seems the analysts dislike each other even more than the animosity among coders and hackers. That's the thing about living in bits and bytes—there's no monopoly on knowledge, it's just a matter of getting there first and then moving forward. Analysts squabble over smatterings of data and what it means, with little progression or contribution to humanity or the profession. Kind of makes me feel sorry for the academic community. The IC—well, outside of ops and cyberland—they're all just engaged in mental masturbation. Coders and hackers, now we're talking substance. You can't reach out and touch your product, but it's damn obvious what works and what doesn't.

"Suggestion on where to start?" My last question for the old man.

"That, ma'am, is your job. I have mine to do." He stood and shuffled out.

The Ops director shut down his slide presentation, a signal we should all go. He was never good at departing words of encouragement. There was no requirement for cheerleading or last words of wisdom. Everyone in the tomb understood what was necessary. Except me. There was a lingering doubt. Are we denying or abetting Navalny's plot? A question no one would answer.

chapter

9

and then the lights went out

montgomery, alabama, 3 september 2025

Must be about noon. Sunlight creeping in around the blinds. A feeling of encroaching heat and humidity even the best air-conditioning could not temper. Just like Mumbai, only her mother would never allow this kind of behavior. She had always insisted Adya rise with the sun and go to bed when the moon shone upon her window, saying, "My children are social beings, not citizens of the dark."

She'd played along, but then graduate school started and Bakshi moved to a small apartment. The day began when she tossed blankets off and wandered to the toilet. Brush your teeth, comb hair, then turn on a stove to heat water for a cup of tea. Her boyfriend, an American expat who claimed India as his new home, always made fun of this dazed expedition into wakefulness."You're the original zombie." His standard joke. She'd offer a shy smile. Occasionally, it was a grin and they would be back in bed. Twisted in the sheets, doing what only young people can accomplish. She sometimes missed his company. But the relationship had ended by her own choosing. It was more important to pursue lessons than love, at least back then.

Five years on she had other thoughts. But now the issue was lucre instead of love. More important to make money than pursue a man. Her parents wanted grandchildren. The thought made her recoil. Children were a burden that interfered with life. Let other people have them. She could always borrow a neighbor's crumb-snatcher for an afternoon as a reminder of why there were no offspring in her house.

Would be nice to find a male counterpart—Montgomery had a fair number of options, including the military officers attending school at Maxwell Air Force Base. Strange as it might seem, the Air Force ran all of its officer professional military education at Maxwell. She encountered a fair number of the students at bars, when she infrequently went out. Just never wanted to commit to a relationship that would interfere with the job. One-night stands were fine. "Use them and lose them," she told one of her new business partners during a buzzed happy hour gathering.

Bakshi was now at 3 September 2025—a Wednesday. Not sure why she kept track of dates; aside from 1 November, nothing else really mattered on a calendar. Worked seven days a week, always had. Fortunately, the boys had taken the business lunch and baseball game in stride. A few snide comments about her "extended vacation," but no bad blood. She made it clear this was a subcontract for a single coder, and then she'd be back. Even expressed a willingness to share her future profits. *That* certainly helped smooth the waters.

Afterwards, she'd delved into Fedor's list, delivered via encrypted email as promised.

Fedor didn't aim low. The top eight left her stunned.

Starting with Gennady Timchenko—Putin's closest confidant. Said to be worth $16 billion. Built his fortune on energy and infrastructure investments. Then there was Arkady Rotenberg. Putin's childhood friend and his longtime judo sparring partner. Supposedly had $3 billion stowed away as a result of lucrative government construction contracts. It kept getting better. Boris Rotenberg, Arkady's brother. Collected a cool billion bucks by corralling almost every contract for the Sochi Olympics. Yuri Kovalchuck—estimated worth, $1.5 billion—was supposedly Putin's personal banker. Igor Sechin served as CEO for Rosneft, the largest Russian oil company—no one would even speculate as to what he was worth. But Sechin was said to be one of Putin's closest advisors.

And that was just the top five.

Kirill Shamalov was Putin's ex-son-in-law and the largest shareholder in Sibur, Russia's petrochemical giant. While Putin didn't spend much time with his daughters, Kirill had "no- knock" access to the Kremlin's front office. Oleg Deripaska was the king of aluminum in Russia, with an estimated net worth in the vicinity of $8 billion. Finally, she discovered Aras Agalarov, worth$ 2.5 billion, all from real-estate scams.

Add two more. Prosecutor General Yuri Chaika. Tied to the owners of the Avilon Automotive Group, a luxury vehicle dealer that received over half a billion dollars in Russian government contracts. Chaika was also associated with the Kushchevskaya crime gang, best described as murder-for-hire. Not exactly the kind of company one expects a prosecutor to have on his guest list.

Top it all off with Alisher Usmanov—one of Russia's most politically influential oligarchs. Maintained close ties to the Kremlin and held stakes in leading media outlets. Served as director general of Gazprom Investment holdings, then sold out for a billion-dollar retirement—after investing a grand total of approximately $200 million. Tidy profit. The son of a bitch went so far as to donate an $85 million mansion in Moscow to a foundation with direct links to Russian prime minister Dmitri Medvedev—Putin's endlessly loyal right-hand man.

All that money... and yet the taxable holdings on file with Russian banks totaled no more than $350 million.

The rest was afloat.

And not sitting in the Caribbean, or on Cyprus. A second round of Panama Papers—that collection of 11.5 million financial documents leaked in 2015—took place in 2023. Revealed what was known of the Russian oligarch holdings—"Not much." The cash sat in cryptocurrency. Fedor knew it. And now, so did Bakshi.

There are only two ways to hold that much money in the cyber world. A "wallet" on your personal computing device—typically not a phone; blockchain burned up too much memory for an online account—or a web wallet.

On the personal side, there are two favorites. A "hardware" wallet is the most secure option. It's an external hard drive specifically designed for storing cryptocurrency. Then there's the "desktop" wallet—a software program installed on your computer's hard drive. The most common type of bitcoin wallet, desktop options were relatively easy to hack.

She knew where the money had gone—"web wallets." Web wallets are hosted on a server outside the house or office. You can access them from any computer; however, that makes them more vulnerable to hackers. Case in point, Mt. Gox, a Bitcoin exchange based in Shibuya, Japan, was plundered to the tune of 850,000 Bitcoins—about $400 million back then—in February 2014. Coincheck was hacked for somewhere in the vicinity of $530 million during January 2018.

Seems crypto crime pays at a pace the traditional bank robber could never match. A ransacking of reporting on traditional theft revealed the largest heist occurred in August 2005, when a team of six to ten thieves tunneled into a bank vault located in Fortaleza, Brazil. They made off with just shy of $70 million—a haul that weighed 3.5 tons. Keystrokes were a lot easier on the spine and required no mucking about in the dirt. Or explosives.

Bakshi was tasked with expropriating billions. Billions. All in the form of computer code. If they could get into the accounts. The good doctor was still uncertain Fedor understood the complexity of this task. While the blockchain for a Bitcoin was only about thirty thousand lines of code, the distribution of "miners" made "N-version programming" a near impossibility. Patching or hacking the current version meant distribution of the "fix" could take days or weeks.

That meant a zero-day vulnerability, remaining on any machine not updated, was still there long after the problem was thought to have been addressed. Conversely, a backdoor might be closed long before she discovered a way in. Maddening.

To this point, her only progress had been in identifying accounts associated with the oligarchs. They simply had so much money pushed into the system it was no longer possible to disguise the transactions. Move $100 million here or $50 million there and even the crypto coverts will start to take notice. Usually in emails to one another. Something to the effect of, "Did you catch the shitload of cash that just came through the system?"

Conversely, that tendency to gossip helped her lock down the blockchain identities of seven of her ten top targets. The last three, Timchenko, Shamalov, and Chaika, were more elusive. Turned out they switched identities within the system. Not once, but twice, each. A pattern indicative of a third party serving to mask transactions. And did so without leaving a trail. Shit, another master hacker. Only this one was clearly on Putin's payroll.

Time to contact Fedor.

After a late-afternoon breakfast with her business partners.

And an exchange of thoughts on who else might be "playing" in their lair. She set up the gathering at Mr. Gus'—best Greek and Italian in Montgomery—and you could get a beer with your omelet and sour dough toast. Leave that whole wheat for health nuts.

Turns out the boys were busy. Hired to transition an Amazon advertisement campaign into a nightmare for the sponsoring firm. Bakshi had to chuckle at their originality. The corporate entity in question—a Korean automobile manufacturer—had designated its latest product the Aram. Sounded cool, was easy for almost anyone to pronounce. Unfortunately, in Amharic it translated into "you shitter."

"Here's the trick," one of them explained to her. "If you go on the web there's a whole set of cool listings for 'Aram,' including a biblical reference to northern Syria. What they failed to check was an odd set of Ethiopian dialects. Needless to say, that's now common knowledge."

The boys had climbed into the Amazon and Google search engine innards and ensured any query for "Aram" immediately came up with the Amharic variant of the vehicle's name. Out of curiosity, she made them explain where this idea had come from.

"Remember the Chevy Nova?"

Of course not, she had no interest in old American automobiles.

"Well, when the geniuses at GM went to sell the Nova in Spanish-speaking countries, they discovered a bastardized pronunciation of 'Nova' meant 'doesn't go.' Didn't impact sales, but it was an object lesson for the advertisement department at every firm looking to operate on an international scale. Apparently not a bit of wisdom passed down in Korean business schools."

"What'd we earn for that bit of mischief?" Her curiosity and the absence of any cash from Fedor caused a financial query.

Grins from across the table.

"The suits at two of the big three paid a hefty $450,000 for four hours of work."

She didn't ask which of the three—Chrysler, Ford, or General Motors—were witting culprits, but she could guess. You couldn't cross the street in Montgomery without risk of being run down by a pickup truck. That meant it was the corporate manufacturers specializing in sedans. Well, at least the business continued to be profitable despite her absence.

"Allow me to describe the problem." She'd folded her hands on the table, omelet gone, a few sips of beer accented with Tabasco dribbling down her throat. Best to stay sober when playing cyber games. "I need a means of shutting down the blockchain for about five minutes."

Pause.

"The Bitcoin blockchain?" Asked in near simultaneous incredulity.

"Yes." Her prime and proper response.

Second pause.

"You have to be fucking me." Business Partner One.

Third time lucky.

"With a hockey stick." Business Partner Two.

"No, I am quite serious. The only way to complete this job is to alter the blockchain records. And, the only way to accomplish that without trying to find a zero-day error is to turn off 51 percent of the miners. Simultaneously."

They just sat and stared at her. Partner One took a large drink of his beer, Partner Two reached across the table, hoisted her glass, and took a large swallow. Followed by significant coughing and a bright red face. He'd forgotten her preference for the Tabasco addition.

"Shit, why can't you just drink a beer without adding curry?" His wheezed comeback.

"No one puts curry in beer." Her curt answer. "Well, you have thoughts?"

Partner One was already on the phone.

Google, mobile search, less likely to catch attention.

Except for a crew working at an obscure section of 1600 Amphitheatre Parkway in Mountain View, California.

Said crew would be the one stationed at Googleplex—a collection of buildings offering 3.1 million square feet of workspace and better connectivity than the children at NSA could ever claim. Little known to most of its consumers, Google monitored search requests. Most of it filtered via AI, but the odd request would be flagged and flashed in front of a human. God forbid the algorithms were not optimized on a nearly daily basis. And then there was that uncomfortable relationship with the U.S. intelligence community.

This one caught the AI filter's attention.

"Location for majority of Bitcoin miners?"

Didn't need the question mark, but he'd included it anyway. Which was the "flag" for Google's alert filter. Regular users didn't bother with a question mark. Wasn't necessary. Employment of such punctuation suggested a neophyte—not many of them left on the planet—or a non-English-speaking query being launched out of the American South.

The answer came back almost as quickly as Bakshi's partner had submitted the request.

"Distributed computing is not correlated with distributed mining."

Dr. Bakshi looked at him for a moment. "I speak English as well, or better, than you two clowns. Explain that phrase."

Partner One came back just as quickly. "Millions of miners, 82 percent parked in China. Want to turn off the blockchain? Turn off the power. In a select set of Chinese cities."

"At what cost to human life?" Her parents, observant, if not terribly practical, Hindus, had taught her the purpose of life is fourfold: to achieve Dharma, Artha, Kama, and Moksha. Dharma, the first purpose, demanded one act virtuously and righteously. She had no reason to explain the remaining three during this conversation.

There was a pause in the back and forth. Not unusual among these three. But, she'd obviously caused a moment's reflection.

Now both partners were thumbing away at their phones.

And Google's security staff had begun to record the requests—linking each subsequent search with the first.

This conversation would most assuredly be passed to NSA.

Bad karma.

Partner Two answered first: "Rough estimate, in a city of twenty-four million—say Beijing or Shanghai—between the traffic accidents, public transportation incidents, and hospital fatalities—let's argue fifteen hundred in the first five minutes. And you're not talking about potential aircraft issues or longer-term consequences of rebooting computers and communications systems. Nor have you considered the impact on the electric grid. Suffice it to say, it's easier to turn off the power than turn it back on."

She must have turned a bit pale.

Partner One asked if Bakshi was feeling well.

"Yes." Her monosyllabic answer.

"Now consider you're turning off power in at least ten major cities—anywhere from five million to twenty-five million residents—all at once and then jumping into the blockchain." Partner One adding to the conversation. "Rough guess ... you kill twelve thousand, all to make a Russian hacker happy."

She threw up on the floor beneath the table. There was insufficient time to run for a bathroom. Bakshi came up looking flushed, obviously had not thought this through. Neither partner made a comment. In the world of professional hacking a sudden acquisition of morals and principles was bad for business.

She took a deep breath. A swallow of beer. "Life is not always fair. There are already too many Chinese."

A comment that drew no reaction from her partners. They understood it was simply a means of justifying her actions. The consequences would be hers to suffer.

chapter 10

all's fair game

washington, dc, 11 september 2025

Thursday, it's a Thursday. Nothing happens on the fourth day of a week in Washington, DC. Trust me, baby. I've been living here long enough to know bad news only gets dumped on Friday afternoon. Preferably about 5 P.M. Too late for the newspapers to update, and the camera boys are already locking in the nightly news. Yeah, you're right, CNN will carry the latest update, but who watches CNN on a Friday night? Even I manage to find a social life on Friday nights—particularly in mid-September. Perfect weather for dining alfresco and touring the streets of this nation's capital.

Anyway, it's Thursday. Thursday at 1930, that would be 7:30 P.M. for those of you who aren't condemned to living in a 24/7 world. And my email accounts go apeshit. First hit comes from my counterpart at NSA. The second one runs out of the counterintelligence boys at CIA. Then it turns into a media feeding frenzy. Anyone who thinks they have a contact worthy of supporting a backstory is dumping shit into my electronic inbox.

Why?

Check this out. A Russian hacker has just dropped two hundred thousand Twitter bot posts aimed at influencing the American elections online. Of course, it's only 340 days after the event, but better late than never. In this case, it's the election that put Chuck

Schumer in the White House and gave the Republicans renewed control of the House and Senate. They lost it back in 2018 (thank you, Donald Trump), but they're back.

And it wasn't just because the Koch brothers spent a fortune on congressional races. Don't get me started on the Supreme Court's ruling on Citizens United versus the Federal Election Commission. The last fifteen years have been witness to more corporate spending in the campaign realm than you can imagine. Back in the day, you know, when Barack was running for the Oval, well, an argument was made we should spend more to elect a president than the annual receipts for dog food. In other words, in 2008, when Obama spent $760,000 to win that front office, Americans disposed of somewhere in the vicinity of $15 billion to feed Fido.

Ain't like that anymore. The presidential race, just the presidential race, in 2024 tallied $6.6 billion. Then you add in the House campaigns and those thirty-three Senate seats. We blew a cool $18 billion on political advertising and sundry other crap. All for one election. The ethics folks were running about with hair afire. To no avail. The corporate bastards bought our legislature; they just missed on the White House. Schumer only won by taking advantage of that pesky institution embedded in the Constitution—yep, the Electoral College. Same way Trump shimmied into 1600 Pennsylvania Avenue.

Anyway, here it is a Thursday evening in September 2025, nearly a year after the fact, and now some Russian decides to release his findings on foreign influence in the 2024 U.S. presidential race.

Go fucking figure.

But don't dodge the facts.

Turns out Moscow knows how to play the cultural and political passions that make Americans tick. Hey, I'm not leaving nobody out. The African-American community has its own share of bigots and racists. Just try being gay or something other than "normal" in the black community. It ain't pretty, baby. Richard Nixon figured that out back in 1968. Hasn't got any better.

Now we're back to my brother's job. Still going to leave you on hold. More important things to discuss. With me?

So, here's what the Russian drops on a Thursday night. I'll just offer a small sampling of the two hundred thousand plus hits this bastard put online.

favorite_count	Text
	RT @mc_derpin: #TheOlderWeGet the more pessimistic we are https://t.co/zS3jHZJl8P
	RT @1_Hoof_Hearted: @TuckerCarlson @JRubinBlogger #Bigot
	I'm a #white #Pence supporter My daughter is half #hispanic I have #AfricanAmeric...
0	RT @stormynights10: #PenceFavoriteHeadline Pence's Lingerie Bedroom Line Collection, with lead model Ivanka Trump
65	#HowToConfuseAMillennial Let them WATCH what Muslims think about women's rights! https://t.co/J994mUkbJl
0	RT @Pamela_Moore13: People starting to wake up! Black Americans Chant 'Schumer Is Racist' Outside Schumer Fundraiser in #Miami https://t.co...
84	#MichelleObama addresses Karen Pence's plagiarism and does a killer impression of Barack #blackgirlsmagic https://t.co/6hygCFL8SH
0	RT @jimmylemons: assisted suicide is legal in Washington state https://t.co/CoQ6hSiE31
	#IfICouldntLie I'd become mute
0	RT @tpartynews: Pence raises $2 billion in small donations in one day!!! Schumer gets millions in donations from foreign countries! https://...
0	How fucked up our country will be if Schumer wins in 2020 and then wins again in 2024 Or vise versa

289 Liberals keep on saying that Islam is peaceful while Muslims firebomb bus in Paris https://t.co/VQ2MHPxikD

0 RT @luvGodncountry: Schumer's Campaign Tries to Turn 'Saint James' Mueller Into Ken Starr | https://t.co/Mrl3rmDMrw

518 Ed Klein: Schumer's spokeswoman couldn't stop crying and blamed Muller_& Pence for not doing enough to stop FBI investigation. https://t.co/bx4ulFhpUf

#HonorForTheBrave If you feel like to be brave and fair then you must become a policeman

18 Schumer never negotiates with terrorists, he gives them what they want https://t.co/prgs9mUtnL

187 #AltRightMeans knowing that too much diversity and globalization can destroy civilization

RT @NetAdvisor: #ThingsHillaryGoogles
How come only Democrat supporters burn the #American flag?
https://t.co/UXs4oeRWLv

1 @ChuckSchumer You belong to PRISON!

RT @ErinLichnovsky: MT @Only1Jaffa: I will remember & honor the ones who died & sacrificed their life for us. https://t.co/sqs4qvLYYy #InHo...

0 RT @travisj0331: #IHaveARightToKnow why @ChuckSchumer deleted those emails.

Service with a smile #UnlikelyThingsHeardAtWalmart

21 Watch: black Pence supporter explains why she is voting for Mike Pence!
Blacks for Pence
#PenceAHorrorMovie https://t.co/BWxNqYXJv6

RT @JohnSWright49: Hangin' out with @BillZucker, @mikeshippey and @Zhangarang at @TheComedyStore on A Friday night! https://t.co/pyQesFcxts...

0 RT @Pamela_Moore13: Jon Voight :"If God allows truth to be said & heard, then we will see Pence as President of this great America." https:...

	RT @cutupx2: Complacency will not give you anymore than what you already have. Change is to take the Risk, without Risk nothing new is ev...
338	While Schumer is busy playing golf our next president is heading to #Louisiana. https://t.co/wWYGVlc6rL
175	There is one thing that we can all AGREE on Schumer MUST BE STOPPED from changing the Supreme Court! Spread this n...https://t.co/tHgFNZz4hf
	RT @CurtisBigMan: #IGetDepressedWhen mom's friends ask me when am I gonna marry
	RT @StevenEveral: A needed bonk to the head so you STFU #SecondhandGifts https://t.co/qMg82jTBjY
0	RT @nananb55: Top Evangelical Theologian Withdraws Support of Mike Pence https://t.co/0gNAK9BJgq #tcot #ccot #NeverPence #NeverSchumer
1184	"Schumer haven't just made money off rich people; they've also figured out how to make money off the poorest of the... https://t.co/XdViAHdNP3
	RT @BreitTwit1: @Time clearly hasn't seen the season finale of Homeland yet. #AngelaMerkel
	If I get a Whammy, we're going to Taco Bell #BigBucksNoWhammies #GameShowHostPickUpLines https://t.co/BdpcmKZHD5
	RT @Relax_For_Real: I'm still alive #UpsideOf2016
0	RT @GroverNorquist: This is why Chuck Schumer opposes education reform, Uber, your right to work, independent contractors--he isn't allo...

You with me now? This shit ain't pretty. And it went on and on, throughout the campaign. But that ain't nothing in comparison to the crap fed into Facebook and Google email. Probably would have given Pence the election, but most Americans have become smart enough to get their primary news feeds from the major providers—

New York Times, Wall Street Journal, Washington Post... CNN, the big three, and NPR.

Same isn't true of people casting ballots in House and Senate elections. They still read and believe the garbage their friends forward on social media. Yeah, deaf leading the blind. That's where the Russian campaign paid dividends. Chuck Schumer can't get shit accomplished. The fucking Republicans are a damn brick wall standing in the path of progress.

Unless your bank account starts with six figures or your last name is Blankfein, Dimon, Koch, Paulson, Mnuchin, or Rubin. Well, guess you could also add Clinton, Obama, Pelosi, Trump, and Schumer. Guaranteed, they walked out of the political world a hell of lot richer than when they went in. Or at least their children inherited a lot more than originally expected.

Ugh, I'm ranting. This Thursday night surprise has taken me off-stride.

What I should be explaining is the cyberworld is now the fifth domain of warfare. Or so the Pentagon likes to claim. You know the first four: air, land, sea, and space. The digital realm, well, that has the kids over at the five-sided disaster wandering about with glazed expressions. Seems someone explained to the brass it was easier to blow things up or turn them off than manipulate data flow and change content.

See, here's the problem. The boys and girls dressed in camouflage, all of whom were raised and trained in an environment where you *owned* the "toys," discovered that's not the case when it comes to the web. Get this, an eye-opener for the military control–mongers. Ninety-nine percent of the electricity they need for operating modern computer comms systems comes from outside providers. Ninety percent of their cables, routers, and other infrastructure? Yep, outside providers.

Hard to secure shit you don't own.

So, they come up with a mission statement. Three parts. Typical DoD... that's Department of Defense; none of us DC insiders call government functions by anything other than the initials. Why waste your breath? All the other inside-the-Beltway types know what you mean.

Here's what they decided CYBERCOM would do before the Oval took it away: (1) run and defend the DoD networks scattered across this entire planet; (2) support the "warfighters" who actually pull triggers or artillery lanyards—see, I can do "milspeak" too; (3) protect the U.S. via what they called the Cyber National Mission Force.

Now there's a joke. According to the old rumors circulated among the CYBERCOM types I work with at CIA, DoD was going to chase an old special operations model and stand up 133 "cyber mission teams." A bunch of airmen, grunts, and sailors that would be specifically trained to wreak havoc on a cyber adversary. No more jamming radars and spoofing communications. No, sir. They were going to go out and conquer the data domain in a manner similar to that employed to dispose of physical impositions.

Right.

They failed at the initial mission right off the bat.

Easier to do defense than offense in the digital world. They screwed the pooch on that mission. Then they blundered into the Chinese operations.

Should have left it to Mandiant. A private firm that spent over a year unraveling Beijing's cyber ops in the U.S. of A. Smart bastards, Mandiant, couple of their team members even came from NSA. Some "wise" senior leader wearing stars—I'd bet, I don't actually know, could have been some sleep-deprived major—decided DoD would go shut down the Chinese.

Like I said, offense is harder than defense in this business. Beijing didn't even bother to issue a diplomatic protest. Instead the PLA (that's the Chinese army) posted the attempted hack, and the associated software, on multiple websites, then suggested America should get a bit of its own lesson.

Ten million Chinese hackers let loose with some of the best code

NSA can write. Yeah, it wasn't pretty. Downloaded and disseminated the contents of almost every congressman or -woman's email. Did the same to the Senate, then hacked into the Supreme Court files. There's so much shit on Wikileaks these days that Julian Assange had to go hire a team of archivists to help sort through the treasure trove. In less than six months, a full tenth of the U.S. Congress resigned, most out of revelations concerning embarrassing affairs or clear evidence of pay-to-play.

Should have known better than to store anything of a personal or sensitive nature on a computer. I still use a note pad. And have a damn good shredder. Nothing with ink on it goes in the trash. Even the crossword puzzle I fight with on Sundays hits the shredder. The only paper that gets recycled here is one that came from a known publisher.

Oh, and Julian? You recall the supposed "wacko" who posted all the material Private Chelsea Manning so thoughtfully passed along. Well, Julian's archivists discovered a trail of emails that revealed his supposed sexual encounters and subsequent criminal charges were all conjured up in a sequence of meetings at the National Security Council. Seems someone at the NSC felt compelled to share notes with a senior legislator on Capitol Hill. Go figure.

Julian is a free man these days. Still collecting embarrassing data and making it available to the world. The only people prohibited from reading his collection? The U.S. intelligence community and anyone wearing an American uniform. Seems their bosses were concerned the mere act of reading this crap would expose a national secret.

I shit you not. The rest of the world has full access.

Now, I'm off track. Back to Thursday night.

There I am answering email. Wondering what they want back at Langley. No clear tasking in anything coming across my desk.

Yet.

Guess I should let you in on another term in our world. "Advanced Persistent Threat." Also just called an APT.

I'm not bragging, but the kids at CIA insist that I am an APT.

Of one. You see, baby, in the computer world, an APT is composed of a team where one group specializes in surveillance—"target development"—a second collective works on "persistent" attacks—think about all those "phishing" emails you get—and the third does the dirty work, system intrusion. Once you're in, I like to use an account from someone in the target's senior management (they don't get as much IT monitoring as the peons), then it's just a matter of locating the right software or implanting the bots before backing out.

If you do it right, the target will never know you were there. Or even worse, at least from a corporate or government perspective, you discover someone has been in the network and likely left behind an unpleasant "present." Six months later. Think "Buckshot Yankee."

Back in 2008, some young analyst at NSA discovered a rogue program operating on a U.S. military network. Remember Conficker? Yeah, that discussion we had a few days back. Apparently sent out a signal to a host computer requesting instructions—what to download, what to shut off, whose files to copy or delete—strange stuff. U.S. government spent a year and a lot of money trying to kill it. Hence Operation Buckshot Yankee. Private industry has the same problems. Can never tell if the intrusion is meant to derail, disable, or steal.

I do it right.

By myself.

And, I don't leave presents that come with a trail. Once I'm in . . . well, you're screwed.

The intel geeks provide all the names and suspect sites. I take care of the rest.

Not as easy as you might think.

Helps to have a home with eleven resident routers and more computing power than the average space platform. Even better to have an employer who pays the electric bill and is willing to fund upgrades with no questions concerning provider or price. But even that won't save your ass. Thanks to the NSA's sloppy security procedures, XKEY-SCORE, a program the agency developed to trace a hacker's location or the machine used to launch an attack, is now available to every swinging dick on the web who knows how to read.

Baby, it's an unfriendly world.

My boss made it just that much less inviting at about 2245 (10:45 P.M.) Thursday evening.

He knows I'm a vampire, so doesn't have any compunction about calling at all odd hours, with the exception of gym time. Even that idiot figured out the sanctity of gym time.

Mr. Sensitive, as always. "Strap on the seatbelt that chair's supposed to have."

"Fuck you." My usual reply. I'm not your model employee.

"Game's changed, the Oval is pissed. Something about 'fucking with American elections.'" Quite the explanation, or lack thereof. Typical for a CIA manager. They make them managers after the individual in question proves to be a shitty analyst or crappy field operative.

"And you want me to do what?"

"Payment in kind." Well, at least he was honest. I knew what that meant. They fuck with our info operations, we do the same to them in turn. "By finishing Putin," he adds.

Whoa, that's a whole different level of unhappiness.

"You have recommendations on where to start?" My best rejoinder. Mind is racing. Was focused on monetary objectives until the email went insane three hours ago.

"Pair the financial with a storyline... a storyline with a lot of followers and comments." He made it sound all so simple.

"When?" What the hell do you ask when you get this kind of tasking? Certainly not "how"? He had no damn idea what I did for a living.

"One November."

Phone went dead. I went to bed. Head hurt too much for more computer time. Be back on that damn set of machines in the morning. After the gym.

chapter 11

loose ends ... no longer

moscow, russia, 16 september 2025

A man of wealth and means should always appear confident. More appropriately, a man who has absconded with absolute wealth, and has the means of dictating almost every eventuality, should appear completely at ease. At least in public.

Vladimir Putin was that man. He was spared the American disgrace of continually begging for political donations and rarely found himself at odds with the legislature. Members of the Russian domestic media feared his penchant for inflicting repercussions—occasionally fatal—so they stayed at arm's distance. The military leadership had watched more than one senior officer depart without a farewell or a pension. Even the oligarchs feared his wrath. Look what happened to Mikhail Khodorkovsky. Once Russia's wealthiest man, he crossed Putin, then spent nine years in jail, was stripped of his billions, and finally fled to Switzerland—with just an estimated $170 million remaining to his name.

Then there was Leonid Nevzlin, supposedly worth $2.2 billion when he fled to Israel in 2003. Once considered the wealthiest Jewish Russian oligarch, he was tried in absentia, charged with conspiracy in the murder of five individuals and stripped of his holdings. Yes, the Permanent Court of Arbitration, eleven years later, ruled he should be appropriately compensated for his financial losses. Well, we all know how much attention Moscow pays to events played out in The Hague.

Putin read the memo concerning the court's finding, folded it into neat quarters, and then deposited the slip of paper into a trash can set beside his desk. Never said a word. Nevzlin, needless to say, never saw a dime of the retribution some Dutch magistrate argued he was due. Foolish Europeans, they still think the Russians operate within the envelope of Western legal niceties. Someone apparently forgot to include an observation on the boundary between Western civilization and social norms that the tsars had imposed on a pack of unruly peasants over the course of a thousand years.

Genghis Khan left more than his DNA behind after sweeping through what was to become modern Russia. He, and his descendants, imposed a legacy of civility that could only be entrusted to a man of strength. Women could rise to a similar prominence—Catherine the Great is a classic case in point—but men of nobility were to be a role model all young Russians learned to respect. Men who ruled with an iron fist and scant interest in human rights or liberal democracy.

Until Nicholas II. Weakness of the flesh and mind. Appropriately, dispatched along with his wife and children. Shot, bayoneted, and/or clubbed to death in Yekaterinburg. A worse fate than that inflicted on Rasputin. Adding insult to injury, the bodies were stripped, mutilated, burned, and deposited in the Koptyaki forest. Such was the price of weakness in Russia. Stalin understood, as did Khrushchev. It was Brezhnev and Gorbachev who forgot.

Putin didn't.

Louis XIV managed the French Empire with practices glossed over in history, given the grandeur that is Versailles. Funny thing about that place—it's that damn big because he made the most important nobles and government servants come live under his roof. Best way to ensure they toed his line. Not a man to be trifled with.

Putin had no interest in living with the oligarchs. He simply made it clear they were completely beholden to him. Drunken behavior was to be excused. Any effort to support political opposition was immediate justification for seizing wealth, deporting families, and imprisonment. Some claimed he'd learned all this in the KGB. Bullshit. Say what you will of his public posturing (the bare-chested pictures, the hunting and motorcycle riding), Putin was well read. A student of history. Russian history.

Contemporary Russian history.

Stalin made no plan for succession. The three men who grasped for power on his death—Georgi Malenkov, Lavrentiy Beria, and Nikita Khrushchev—had all fallen out of favor with Stalin after World War II. Khrushchev won the title by virtue of bureaucratic scheming and a demonstrated ferocity behind closed doors. Most Westerners forgot it was Khrushchev who served on the front lines at Stalingrad as the political commissar—the intermediary between Stalin and his generals tasked with the eventual slaughter of approximately 1.2 million Germans and their allies, to say nothing of the 1.1 million dead Russians. All for one city.

Putin was equally reticent in suggesting a successor. Dmitry Medvedev was a useful sycophant, but would not survive the backroom politics and outright bloodshed that could follow Putin's departure. In other words, Medvedev was no Khrushchev. That role Putin assigned to a man who had been tested in fire. A political version of Stalingrad.

He'd selected Alexei Navalny.

And put the man through every test a modern politician could conjure. Including beatings and prison time.

Navalny bounced back. Again and again. Even developed enough spine to recruit allies who apparently were equally intent on disposing of Putin and establishing links to the American political tricksters—fucking International Republican Institute.

Vladimir Putin knew about all of it—including Fedor Ivanov.

Specifically told the SVR and internal security goons to let those connections pass without notice.

If Navalny was going to survive the backstabbing that would follow Putin's departure, he would need connections. More importantly, he would need to suffer adversity. Hence the banishment to that shitty office on New Arbat Street. It was a further element in the "development process." Learn to do without, before being granted the reins of power. Kept, as the Westerners liked to say, hungry. A hungry man is cunning.

Shit, Putin even knew about the IRI plan to derail the oligarchs. He wrote the draft email—we'll come back to that in a moment. What he didn't know was how it could be accomplished. His days of jailing or exiling that lot were coming to an end. He was, in many ways, just as vulnerable. "Better to be feared than loved." That was Machiavelli's argument. Putin was certainly feared, but there was nowhere for him to go from here. The usual refuges were out. He refused to consider Saudi Arabia, and the French would not have him. There was always the possibility of an island in the Caribbean—he had no interest in hiding in oblivion. Too much like Napoleon's fate, a gilded version of Saint Helena. Hell no. For Putin, it was to be a well-appointed dacha outside Moscow and a live-in security team. He could serve as senior counsel and make the ruling bastards come crawling to him. A glorious retirement, replete with fawning admirers.

What he didn't know about was the unexpected inclusion of Dr. Bakshi.

The best-laid plans of mice and men often go awry.

Old line, stolen from Robert Burns. He put it in a poem back in 1785. Still applied today. Hell, Steinbeck borrowed it in 1937 for *Of Mice and Men.* No equivalent in Russian. But in this case one might utter, "*Da! Spasibo bol'shoe!*" (Shit happens!) Little difference; Putin had put the plan into effect ten years ago. Now it was coming to fruition.

He never personally spoke with Navalny. Too great a risk of intercept. Nor could he meet with the man. Any pictures or rumor among staff would bring the whole plot to ruin.

Instead, they worked through "seconds." Trusted agents who had a vested interest in both men's future. Navalny used his ever-suffering secretary. Putin employed a rising SVR agent who sought control over broader elements of the agency. In other words, a man who ultimately sought to follow in Putin's footsteps.

The two "seconds" met for "dinners," and occasionally were "friends with benefits." The gossip was always politics and always about their bosses—but there was never an exchange of names nor formal acknowledgment of the other's position. They met at second-rate restaurants in Moscow and screwed at cheap hotels. Even the Americans were not on to this arrangement.

Until the automobile accident.

Da! Spasibo bol'shoe!

The dispatch of several ambulances to what should have been a routine fender-bender caught the attention of those pesky algorithms driving NSA collection. The COMINT spooks are always ambulance-chasing. Some of the best intelligence comes from an unintended incident. Think Chappaquiddick.

The Russians would never have hooked their claws into Teddy Kennedy had he not drowned the young lady, and CIA would not have landed Benjamin Netanyahu had he managed to avoid certain Hollywood producers.

The list was endless.

Now there were two more names. Known, for the moment, only to Putin, Navalny, and a select set of analysts sitting at NSA and then CIA. Shit happens.

It took the American spooks a couple of months to assemble the entire picture. What emerged was a realization that Navalny's supposed opposition was simply his means of earning Putin's respect.

And that Putin had plans to use Navalny, much as Stalin had employed Lavrentiy Beria. Beria was the head of Soviet security and the secret police during World War II. He was tasked with running the gulags and then set up *sharashkas,* the secret detention sites used to house scientists and engineers.

Stalin trusted Beria to the point he put this former security administrator in charge of the Soviet Union's budding nuclear program. The problem was that when Stalin died, Beria became power-hungry. Was appointed to first deputy premier. Tried to be a member of the troika bidding to run the entire show, but forgot to pay attention to the master politician—Khrushchev. Once in power, Nikita had Beria arrested, charged with treason, and executed.

Putin shared that story with Navalny through their intermediaries. Just to ensure Navalny understood what could happen should the attorney try to outmaneuver the former KGB operative. Message sent, and clearly understood. Navalny worked within parameters dictated from the Kremlin. As such, when Navalny leaked paperwork or produced YouTube documentaries on corrupt oligarchs, it was at Putin's bidding. Same was true of Navalny's periodic public uprisings. Directed from Putin's desk.

While he was certainly no democrat, Putin realized that many Russians—at least the educated, sober members of the supposed Russian electorate—desired a sense of political efficacy. Feed the beast and it will likely stay away from your castle. He allowed Navalny to feed the beast. And then only suffer nominal consequences. Enough prison time, obvious bruising, and occasional police searches of the "opposition" work spaces to keep Putin's inner circle from becoming suspicious.

A subtle game. Louis XIV managed to quell dissent by putting the greatest threat under his roof. Putin accomplished the same feat with his *okruzheniya* via creative destruction. A lesson learned from dealing with Khodorkovsky and Nevzlin those many years ago. Endless press attention and a public perception that the two men were sacrificial victims. He'd never made that mistake again. Nor did he resort to the violent tactics employed in the purported Chechen bombings of four Moscow apartment complexes in 1999. (Let it be said, despite the Western press reports of KGB complicity in the bombings as a means of ensuring Putin's rise from prime minister to president, there was no evidence—including the agents tasked with accomplishing that mission—remaining to be found.)

He'd grown wiser.

The danger of an inner circle populated with wealthy men is a tendency for one, two, or even three members to grow weary of just collecting cash and turn their attention to accumulating political power. Look at Washington, DC. Donald Trump surrounded himself with millionaires and billionaires. They rewarded him with backstabbing, press leaks, and endless squabbling. Putin was not about to suffer such shit.

So, he found Navalny. And a few select reporters who could be counted upon to leak unfavorable accounts of child molestation, corruption, or simple graft—stealing from the public coffers to pad one's own pocketbook. Worked better than he ever expected. In fact, Chinese President Xi Jinping once pulled him aside at Davos, that Swiss gathering of the rich and famous, to ask how Putin managed his inner circle. The Chinese leader returned to Beijing and immediately followed suit.

This time was different. Putin wanted out and he wanted Navalny in.

That meant splintering the *okruzheniya.*

Permanently.

Navalny would have to acquire his own eunuchs. First, however, he would need to clean house. The best means, as far as Putin could imagine, was to start taking away their fortunes. A maneuver he could no longer accomplish. The money was offshore in places even the SVR seemed unable to locate.

Until they stumbled upon the cryptocurrency gambit. Bastards had sunk their fortunes into Bitcoin and then gone into hiding somewhere in the cloud.

Then his "second" suddenly became the voice of IRI on Navalny's Tor-accessed accounts.

Putin would have pushed the SVR into working this problem set, but any trace of his hand could immediately trigger a coup, focused on removing him before he was ready to go. Thus, the pass to Navalny, who Putin knew, would go to Fedor. Fucking Fedor was a pain in the ass.

SVR knew about Endless Horizons; they also knew about Fedor's passionate distaste for Putin. Navalny filled them in on that bit of history. What the SVR knew, Putin knew.

There were quite a few stories about trying to bring Fedor's web days to an end. Even conversation of a fatal "accident." Proposed operations that never won approval in the front offices of the Federal Security Service (FSB)—Moscow's agency charged with internal security and counterintelligence. A Russian variant of the American FBI, only with fewer legal hurdles to clear.

What the FSB did not understand was that Fedor's Endless Horizons proved useful for Putin and his *okruzheniya.* What the Russian anti-alcohol campaign had taken away, Fedor provided. An alternative means of keeping a significant number of would-be troublemakers pacified. Via narcotics. Opioids, meth, heroin, pick the pills of your choice. Endless Horizons was a pacifier for Moscow's twenty-something "intellectual" community.

The one FSB attempt to hack into Endless Horizons proved a disaster. All the FSB servers were off-line for three days. One in every ten computers at headquarters suddenly no longer functioned, at all. There were no electronic fingerprints. But, it was obvious to FSB agents assigned the Fedor file. They could fuck with him, and he would return the favor—in a nuclear manner.

More puzzling had been the sudden firing of their boss. Rumored to have been directed from the Kremlin. Fedor took care of Navalny,

Navalny met Putin's needs, and Putin made the final call on any operation that might interfere with that relationship. Fedor just figured he'd pushed back hard enough to deter the security goons. Truth of the matter—the very man he pledged to destroy was covering Fedor's ass.

Remember this is Russia—a plot, within a plot, within a plot.

Meanwhile, unbeknownst to Putin or Navalny, the Americans were now recording all communications between the two parties. The "seconds" proved to be quite chatty—and Navalny's secretary found the CIA payments a nice supplement to her paltry salary. She had the dead-drop and coffee shop chats down to a fine art.

A plot, within a plot, within a plot.

chapter

12

and then the lights went out

montgomery, alabama, 21 september 2025

Sunday in Montgomery is a quiet event. The churches are full, streets empty, and much of the after prayer and coffee gossip time is given to heavy late lunches. The family gathers around a table laden with Grandma's best cooking, Dad's pulled pork, or a bucket of fried chicken. Then men retire to watch a sports game on TV, kids get to dive back into the internet, and women retreat to wash dishes and lament in the kitchen. It's a vision of the American South only fondly recalled once you travel farther north than Kentucky or Tennessee. Perhaps we could make an exception for West Virginia.

Dr. Bakshi was doing none of the above. She saw little reason to indulge in worshipping false idols. Probably a consequence of being raised by two college professors. Had no taste for American "comfort food," and did not own a television. Anything she wanted to watch could be pulled off Netflix or Amazon Prime. At any time of night or day. She kept up with the news by running NPR in the background and periodically scanning the *New York Times.*

Blinds in her apartment never opened. Most of the lights, with the exception of a bedside lamp and a hooded fixture on her desk, were forever off. Bakshi tried to remember to go for a walk every day, always good to get fresh air. But even that pledge was frequently forgotten. The one luxury she allowed herself was the purchase of a curved 49-inch, high-definition computer monitor. Then configured it so that all three of her machines displayed in split-screen options simultaneously. Took some programming time and more than a bit of cable and connector manipulation. But now the world was at her fingertips without having to glance from machine to machine.

She'd gone so far as to acquire a switch box controlled by verbal commands. That left her with a desk stretching ten feet across the wall of her designated "office," a space intended to be a second bedroom. She never had guests—the office was now her woman cave. Three laptops ran at one end of a wood slab sitting atop sawhorses. They fed the monitor and allowed for access to multiple websites at any given time. She Bluetoothed a keyboard to the switch box. Purchased the best damn one she could find. If you spend all your waking hours typing... well, a real mechanic requires the best tools.

Spent a lot of time learning about SCADA.

SCADA, Supervisory Control and Data Acquisition, is the means by which human operators and, increasingly, AI, control physical equipment. Perhaps, most infamously, power plants, but also gas pipelines and even metal detectors at an airport. SCADA software links the 5,800 power plants that keep America air-conditioned and cell phones charged. The software is notoriously outdated and poorly protected. And that's in the United States.

Stuxnet, the virus unleashed on Iran's uranium enrichment facility, was a SCADA attack. Moscow upped the game in 2015 by going after the Ukrainian power grid. These days SCADA was a ready target. Everyone knew it. The problem was expense. Even after the U.S. Department of Homeland Security demanded that electrical providers upgrade... some did, a lot more did not. Too costly to upgrade all the software on a variety of aging equipment. Even if you could foot the bill, there was no guarantee that pimple-faced IT employees would know how to complete the work.

Which meant the legacy software with all its faults remained a constant—in America.

She could only imagine the nightmare facing New Delhi. The Indian power grid was best described as cobbled together with duct tape and bailing wire. Not her problem.

Her problem resided on the northern side of the Himalayas. China. More specifically, she was chasing the power grids feeding Beijing, Chengdu, Chongqing, Guangzhou, Hangzhou, Jinan, Shanghai, Tianjin, Wuhan, and Xian. Metropolitan areas with a combined population of 214 million people. And approximately 70 percent of the Chinese Bitcoin miners.

The trick was shutting down the world's largest electric grid. Beijing had compelled the formation of two synchronous grids back in 2005, but had little success in enforcing software upgrades at the more than seven thousand plants feeding juice into the system. It was a patchwork of modernity and decrepit coal-burning facilities with one common weakness: SCADA had to be able to work with them all.

Talk about old software. She'd bet the kids at CYBERCOM had learned long ago how to accomplish what she needed to do for a scant five to ten minutes, *without* causing a war.

That problem had come to haunt her after reading through a collection of U.S. policies concerning a perceived—or even worse, detected—strike on the national power grid. In an application of "smart power" proactive deterrence, the Pentagon had announced such an event would be considered an attack on the homeland and would unleash the wolves. Beijing made no such proclamation. Typical for China. Plan to bite without the decency of at least barking a warning.

Here was the trick. Back in August 2003, a vast majority of the northeast American power grid went offline for up to forty-eight hours. Impacted 50 million people, was blamed for the death of eleven. The White House declared it wasn't terrorism and the electric companies claimed it was a "power surge" caused by excessive demand due to a heat wave. Then it was supposedly a power line rubbing tree branches in Ohio.

Slippery answers.

Bakshi was an academic. She'd done the homework. It was a SCADA attack. Probably some geek in Russia or else some sixteen-year-old punk in Pittsburg. No way to tell, the forensic trail was way too cold. The power companies hadn't bothered to retain electronic records of the event. They just blamed the trees in Ohio and went back to peddling electricity. Even the feds bought that forestry explanation.

But that was twenty-two years ago. Washington was no longer so forgiving.

Beijing, she quickly discovered, was less observant. At least when it came to the crypto domain. Yes, the Chinese had tried to stamp out the cryptocurrency campaign, with no success. And, yes, Beijing repeatedly upgraded the "Great Firewall," only to be immediately defeated by a legion of coders. Google remained locked out of the People's Republic, as was Amazon. But Baidu and Alibaba were making money hand-over-fist. Why bother with the pesky Westerners?

All of which caused her to do a little shopping. On Shodan.

Launched in 2003—starting to see connections here?—Shodan was a website that crawled through the World Wide Web stalking SCADA systems. For a minor fee, the service sent you the most recently discovered systems currently operating through the internet to control everything from wind turbines to backup generators. For a bit more cash, all in Bitcoin, you could have the data sorted by country and technology. For significantly more money, Shodan was known to part with the expertise necessary to access the systems you had selected.

Bakshi had the money. Fedor proved true to his word. Her online Bitcoin wallet seemed to have no limit. Even was good at the local Winn-Dixie grocery store.

She selected to test the software on Chifeng, a city of 1.3 million souls in inner Mongolia. Proved frighteningly easy to switch everything off seven thousand miles west of her desk. Then she made the mistake of watching the recovery operations. Learned a painful lesson about electrical grids and the potential consequences of her next step.

What most people do not realize is that while it's relatively easy to take a grid off-line, it's a genuine work of art to start the damn thing back up. Think of electricity like water. If you dam a stream the flow will cease, everything below the structure goes dry. But if you knock down that dam with a sudden gesture, well, the villages downstream flood and things get broken.

The same is true of electricity. Contrary to the Hollywood movie depictions, there is no giant on-off switch at the local power plant. Once the juice stops flowing, you have to turn it back on in a methodical process. Otherwise transformers blow and power lines fry. Fuses are resident at every business and household power supply point of origin to protect against just such a contingency.

What Bakshi accomplished from her desk at 0135 in the morning, her time, was at 1535 (3:35 P.M.) in Chifeng. She'd planned this figuring that mid-afternoon should minimize the potential for disaster in the Chinese city. What she presumed would take fifteen minutes to correct took the Chinese twenty-one hours. And all she'd done was shut down the grid; there was no attempt to destroy equipment or permanently disable control functions. Watching the news reports, the good doctor discovered her "little experiment" had cost fourteen lives. Primarily in automobile accidents and hospital patients on artificial respiration. But, she also killed three linemen charged with repairing equipment and lines damaged during the return of electricity across the sprawling city.

Do the math. If an outage in a city of 1.3 million caused fourteen deaths, at best she could expect to murder just under three thousand when she went after the blockchain miners in the top ten population centers. Hell of a lot better than the twelve thousand she'd originally estimated. Now it was just philosophical rationalization—one death is a tragedy, three thousand are a statistic. It was a cold academic rationalization. One that would have left her parents in despair at the child they'd raised.

Time to contact Fedor.

After she figured out how to break into the blockchain.

The answer came at 0100 on a sleepless night. In the coding world, respectable cryptology scrambles the protected text in a manner that renders it random keystrokes for prying eyes. In theory—remember this is theory, as is all encryption—the original plain-text (what you would see on a screen at work or home when using a word-processing program) is rendered unrecognizable for someone not in possession of the decryption key—software these days.

That's the theory. Here's the weakness in blockchain; the format of the blocks is well-known and relatively easy to decipher. There are numbers, letters, and characters in the same places in every block. Which, by the way, identify the owner and the transaction. Once you crack that code, the block and all associated transactions are changed across the entire transaction process. You just had to shut down that magic 51 percent of the blockchain participants to initiate the revised string of transactions on the remaining machines.

She'd figured out how to turn off the 51 percent.

Now it was a matter of cracking the SHA-256.

Fedor understood what she was combating, very few other people did. SHA-256 (Secure Hash Algorithm-256) creates a 256-bit…32-byte hash. A hash is a one-way function. There is no means of decrypting one of these on a return cycle.

SHA-256 was the black magic behind a blockchain.

It was a NSA invention. In ordinary English—it's too easy to fall into geek-speak on this stuff—acryptologic function employs a numeric algorithm to compare a generated hash with a known and expected hash. If they match, the incoming "package" is considered valid. Miss the hash test, and that new batch of data is ether toast. Lost to the bit and byte gods. Think of it this way; by examining the hash of an incoming package with a previously published hash you—or, more appropriately, the software—can determine if the new "package" has been modified or manipulated.

Years before she'd sketched out on an explanation of this process on a whiteboard. Course requirement for one of the classes in her doctorate program in information technology. Made perfect sense to the fellow programmers, less so to a visiting group of enrollees in a political science methodology class. They went glass-eyed.

She could still scribble out the logic. Looked like this:

h0: = 0x6a09e667
h1: = 0xbb67ae85
h2: = 0x3c6ef372
h3: = 0xa54ff53a
h4: = 0x510e527f
h5: = 0x9b05688c
h6: = 0x1f83d9ab
h7: = 0x5be0cd19

Initialize array of round constants:
(first 32 bits of the fractional parts of the cube roots of the first 64 primes 2.311):
k[0.63]: =
0x428a2f98, 0x71374491, 0xb5c0fbcf, 0xe9b5dba5, 0x3956c25b, 0x59f111f1, 0x923f82a4, 0xab1c5ed5,
0xd807aa98, 0x12835b01, 0x243185be, 0x550c7dc3, 0x72be5d74, 0x80deb1fe, 0x9bdc06a7, 0xc19bf174,
0xe49b69c1, 0xefbe4786, 0x0fc19dc6, 0x240ca1cc, 0x2de92c6f, 0x4a7484aa, 0x5cb0a9dc, 0x76f988da,
0x983e5152, 0xa831c66d, 0xb00327c8, 0xbf597fc7, 0xc6e00bf3, 0xd5a79147, 0x06ca6351, 0x14292967,
0x27b70a85, 0x2e1b2138, 0x4d2c6dfc, 0x53380d13, 0x650a7354, 0x766a0abb, 0x81c2c92e, 0x92722c85,
0xa2bfe8a1, 0xa81a664b, 0xc24b8b70, 0xc76c51a3, 0xd192e819, 0xd6990624, 0xf40e3585, 0x106aa070,

0x19a4c116, 0x1e376c08, 0x2748774c, 0x34b0bcb5, 0x391c0cb3, 0x4ed8aa4a, 0x5b9cca4f, 0x682e6ff3,
0x748f82ee, 0x78a5636f, 0x84c87814, 0x8cc70208, 0x90befffa, 0xa4506ceb, 0xbef9a3f7, 0xc67178f2

Pre-processing:
begin with the original message of length L bits
append a single "1" bit
append K "0" bits, where K is the minimum number > = 0 such that L + 1 + K + 64 is a multiple of 512
append L as a 64-bit big-endian integer, making the total postprocessed length a multiple of 512 bits

Process the message in successive 512-bit chunks:
break message into 512-bit chunks
for each chunk create a 64-entry message schedule array w[0.63] of 32-bit words
(The initial values in w[0..63] don't matter, so many implementations zero them here)
copy chunk into first 16 words w[0..15] of the message schedule array

Extend the first 16 words into the remaining 48 words w[16.63] of the message schedule array:
for I from 16 to 63
s0: = (w[i-15] rightrotate 7) xor (w[i-15] rightrotate 18) xor (w[i-15] rightshift 3)
s1: = (w[i-2] rightrotate 17) xor (w[i-2] rightrotate 19) xor (w[i-2] rightshift 10)
w[i]: = w[i-16] + s0 + w[i-7] + s1

Initialize working variables to current hash value:
a: = h0
b: = h1
c: = h2
d: = h3
e: = h4
f: = h5
g: = h6
h: = h7

Compression function main loop:
for I from 0 to 63
S1: = (e rightrotate 6) xor (e rightrotate 11) xor (e rightrotate 25)
ch: = (e and f) xor ((not e) and g)
temp1: = h + S1 + ch + k[i] + w[i]
S0: = (a rightrotate 2) xor (a rightrotate 13) xor (a rightrotate 22)
maj: = (a and b) xor (a and c) xor (b and c)
temp2: = S0 + maj

h: = g
g: = f
f: = e
e: = d + temp1
d: = c
c: = b
b: = a
a: = temp1 + temp2

Add the compressed chunk to the current hash value:
h0: = h0 + a
h1: = h1 + b
h2: = h2 + c
h3: = h3 + d
h4: = h4 + e
h5: = h5 + f
h6: = h6 + g
h7: = h7 + h

Produce the final hash value (big-endian):
digest: = hash: = h0 append h1 append h2 append h3 append h4 append h5 append h6 append h7

Here's how it translated for the political science visitors. Once you sent an electronic "package" into the blockchain, it could not come back. It might be rejected, and was certainly going to be run through the computing wringer.

Unless you changed "history" and inserted enough "packages" at nearly the same time. Hence the 51 percent rule . . . and acceptance of the fact that three thousand people were likely to perish out of that ambition.

She sighed. It no longer made her sick to think about the consequences of her tasking, just sad.

chapter 13

some stains don't come out in the wash

washington, dc, 22 september 2025

There's some shit you don't want to know about until the weekend comes to a halt.

As usual I come back from the gym, Monday is a "heavy" day for me, I'm feeling refreshed. Ready for another cup of coffee and a strike at the email before heading off to the "Dog Pound." That's what I called the Ops conference room these days. Hey, if I'm the Veterinarian, then I must be running some kind of pet hotel.

But this place was certainly no animal hospital. More than a fair number of our clients came out on the wrong end of mortality. Would have been bad for business if word got out that my hands—or worse yet, one of the staff—killed Fido or Miss Kitty on purpose. Now, don't get me wrong, aside from the jihadi types who seem to want their own death, the CIA is pretty good about minimizing casualties. Shit, in comparison to the SVR, we're positively tame. Go ask the Chechens or Georgians if you don't believe me.

Anyway, "animal hospital" was out, so was "animal shelter." We sure as hell were not gathering all this analytic expertise, collection capability, and computing skill to "shelter" anything. The goal was to contain. Put Putin in a box. Try not to repeat the mistakes of the 2016 U.S. presidential election.

Too bad, I've had a lot of fun creating personalities and organizational listings on Russian Facebook postings over the last eight years. Like I said to one of the congressional types we had to brief on that program, "don't get mad, get even." Congresswoman went on her way with a grin, and there was way more money in that program's budget the following year. I told you, I didn't get promoted to this level just because I'm black, good-looking, and handicapped. Baby, I *know* how to play the political game just as well as I can code. Might want to keep that in mind. Just saying.

Back to where I was headed. Name of the Ops conference room.

I came in for our usual gathering about ten days after this fun and games commenced, looked around the room at a collection of rumpled suits, the pots of burned coffee, a collection of junk food, and declared, "This is the Dog Pound." Must have stuck because the kids in graphics—you should see the CIA graphics department—well, they came in with a slick sign and a logo for my operation's workspace and its occupants.

Big fucking sign. In bloodred lettering reads: The Dog Pound. The associated logo is also cool. Has a pair of Russian wolfhounds staring though eight lines of barbed wire. Did some homework on the wolfhound, apparently a mix of Alaskan malamute and Canadian wolf. Has eyes that peer into your soul and weighs about 120 pounds. (Yeah, yeah, spare me, I know the real Russian wolfhound is called a Borzoi—looks like a hairy greyhound—too wimpy for my team.)

Why the eight strands? Well, by now we've got CIA, CYBERCOM, DIA, FBI, INR, NGA, NSA, and Treasury working on this problem. Eight agencies, eight strands. Told you the kids in graphics were good. The dogs were gray-backed with gray around the nose, the background is that same damn red they used for the sign. Said it was to represent Russia. I had them make up about a hundred stickers the dimension of a good-sized coffee cup and handed them out as "calling cards." A little team/morale building. Also helped when you had to beat on some bureaucrat's door to borrow resources.

Yes, managers are that shallow. In almost every institution. Think I'm lying, get to know some of the Army special forces types. They have all sorts of shit to hand out as a means of acquiring favors. What pencil-necked, desk-bound intel type wouldn't kill to get some of *that* shit hanging over their cubicle?

You people got things to learn about politics. *Told* you, I know this game.

So, there I am on a Monday morning in mid-September. The heat has finally broken, and humidity seems to be on the wane. Not that it really matters to me. Don't spend a lot of time walking around the block or gardening. My brother's kids take care of Wiper. I take care of my brother. Still haven't told you what he does. It can wait. A little longer.

I roll into the workspace at my usual 0930. That gives the team time to prepare their thoughts and check message traffic. Typically, someone will have turned on the three TVs—they run muted all day—and classical music is playing in the background. I've always been a fan of white noise; let the analysts choose what they want to hear all day. As long as it doesn't have lyrics. Can't think when someone starts singing at me.

Today, at least when I arrive, the coffee smells fresh and one of the analysts has gone down to the cafeteria to acquire a selection of bagels and cream cheese spreads (CIA has the best cafeteria in the IC, trust me). I look around, desktops have been shuffled into a semblance of order and the vacuum cleaner was finally turned on—probably for the first time since we took over the room.

"All this for me?" I ask with a bit of sarcasm. I know better. Some stuffed shirt is in-bound.

My deputy walks over. "Ops chief is bringing in the director and that clown who claims to be the DNI."

"Why?" I try to avoid the immediate attack. They should have told me about this days ago. No one gets the new DNI to leave his building without a lot of begging. And he sure as shit knows he's not welcome at CIA.

A bit of stammering from my deputy immediately puts me on edge. "Seems, seems, on Saturday the director went down to the Oval for his usual gossip over the Presidential Daily Briefing."

"Nothing new there." Old story, president selected the current director, they're old acquaintances—friend would be too strong a word in Washington. The director, whenever possible, always personally sat through the president's read of the PDB. And then fielded questions or took notes to bring home taskings. Kind of like Donald Rumsfeld's infamous "snowflakes." You never, ever, wanted one of the director's notes from the PDB to land on your desk. That meant "drop everything and run like a monkey." Because there had to be an answer before he returned to the White House the next morning.

"Yes, so he went to the Oval on Saturday, what's that got to do with us?"

Now my deputy is sweating. Not good. "He briefed Schumer on Operation Dog Pound. Now the president has more questions and demanded the DNI be pulled into our interagency campaign."

Fuck, that meant we were about to get one more level of management. And a lot more attention from the seventh floor.

"You were going to tell me all this when?" I admit, that did probably come across as angry black woman, but I was pissed. If the bear is getting ready to enter your cave it's nice to be armed. At least with some eye candy.

I'll give the man credit; my deputy stood his ground. "Now. You didn't need to worry about this before now. No one knows the mission and results better. Just walk them through, slowly. I don't think the Ops boss has been keeping the director informed of our regular briefings."

There's balls, called me out right there on the spot and then applied intellectual balm to sooth my incensed soul. Touché.

"When?" Time to get the plan in place.

"You should be ready in, oh, say, five minutes." He actually had the audacity to smile at me. "I'm firing up the last presentation we did for the Ops chief and then it's an informal with you and the analysts fielding questions. My bet, most of them come from the director. The DNI and he don't get along. Means the DNI will stick to platitudes so as to avoid revealing his ignorance."

"Thank you. Good read on the coming chaos." I tried to sound polite in that response. Then I whipped the chair around and rolled into the new cubicle they'd put up to serve as my on-site workplace.

Here's another thing I learned from those overpriced business consultants they bring in here for training purposes: "If you wait until the last five minutes, it will only take five minutes." Sounds trite, something a college student would say. In the real world, it's the truth. Another bit of wisdom from that consultant, "Don't worry about what you can't change, it will happen anyway. Put that energy to work on a means of coming out of the situation in the best possible position."

Roger that.

Scrolled through the "night notes" my team had assembled. Not much that was new. Fedor was back to communicating with an unknown entity in the United States. Navalny had released another of his infamous YouTube documentaries with more flashy images of Russian oligarchs flaunting their wealth and political indiscretions. Yawn, could have predicted all this crap without standing up an eight-person watch that churned through the intelligence, internet, and media feed 24/7. Waste of money as far as I was concerned. The Ops chief had requested otherwise.

As you might predict, the director and DNI were running behind schedule, by thirty minutes. I kept waiting for that phone call from the harried secretary in his front office. "Briefing's off, boss has other priorities." It didn't happen.

Thirty-five minutes after they were supposed to arrive, the

"dignitaries" appeared. Employing a shitty Beltway trick. Let people think they're too important to be bothered with whatever trivial matter occupies eight, ten, fourteen hours of your day. Fuckers.

Time to ruin their day.

"Gentlemen, have a seat." Don't like these old white guys hovering over my head while carrying on a conversation. Learned long ago to make sure my "inadvertent" run-ins with the high and mighty took place in locales with chairs they could occupy. That meant I was looking in their eyes, not at their crotches or inevitable guts. Seriously, we need to put the seniors in our government on a mandatory exercise program. Otherwise, you and I get to pay the increased health costs when one of the bastards drops to his knees in the midst of a heart attack. Don't get me going on this topic.

"Welcome to Operation Dog Pound." First slide was our logo with a time stamp to show the last time the slides were updated. Another trick for keeping the boss at bay, make sure they think you are on top of the situation, right down to the minute. Easiest change to make to a PowerPoint presentation, not sure why more people don't learn this bit of manage-the-manager tomfoolery. Hey, I got to save my team, and my ass first. Go learn this shit the hard way on your own.

"Dog Pound started as an initiative prompted by a phone call from Alexei Navalny. Believe you are familiar with Navalny, been serving as Putin's opponent for the last fifteen years. An attorney with political ambitions and a good deal of public support. Also happens to be on our payroll. A decision he made back in 2011, when it appeared Putin was about to wrap up Navalny's operation and then have the lawyer disappear."

I barely take a breath.

"Turns out Navalny's a double agent. Working with us when it's to his advantage, and also in Putin's pocket. Perhaps that's too timid an expression. He's being groomed to take Putin's office. In 2026."

The DNI stopped me. "You know this how?"

"We own Navalny's secretary. That is a strict need-to-know, sir."

An unnecessary gibe, but the son of bitch had a reputation for leaking secrets that got people killed. Some people will do anything for publicity or a chance at further promotion. No secret the DNI would rather be director of the Central Intelligence Agency (DCIA). Not happening anytime soon, if you asked me. He was too much of a dick sucker.

"Navalny and Putin have worked out a bargain. Putin wants the inner-circle of oligarchs to disintegrate. He's reached the point where 'retirement' is more appealing than governance. At least from the Kremlin. As best we can tell, the man remains intellectually sharp and physically fit. Suspect he simply wants to sit in the backroom and pull strings. A lot less stress, and he has the funds necessary to afford a lifestyle I can't even imagine."

I had their complete attention at this point.

"We know back in mid-August Navalny contacted Fedor Ivanov, hacker extraordinaire, for what has proved to be their usual monthly meeting. Fedor has history with Putin ... or at least Fedor's father had history with Putin. Bad history, the fatal kind. Fedor is looking for revenge. Found it by lashing up with Navalny. Now he's willing to put his hacking services to Navalny's use at the drop of a hat."

"Great, another fucking Russian hacker," the DNI sighed, adding his "wisdom" to the conversation.

"Not quite that simple. Navalny, working under Putin's direction, instructed Fedor to go after the oligarchs' wealth. Much of which rests in cryptocurrency. Those bastards learned in a hurry to hide the money from Putin and us. Tough nut to crack, so Fedor went in search of assistance."

"We know who?" The director filling in his own gaps.

"No, sir. NSA believes it is a woman, possibly Indian or Pakistani. My bet is Indian, the Indian Institutes of Technology produce some of the best coders in the world. Go look at the workforce at Microsoft or anywhere in Silicon Valley. She seems to be an independent actor—working somewhere out of the United States. Fedor is careful, any contact they have is done on a disposable cell phone. We have not been able to track an email connection. NSA is working that."

"She can get into the cryptocurrency world?" DNI jumping back in.

"Good question, sir. It can be done, we know that. Been enough thefts from the Bitcoin wallets over the years to suggest there are zero-day holes in the software, but to pull off this task you have to go after the blockchain, and that's a hell of a lot harder."

"Can we monitor attempts to get into the blockchain?" Director of CIA taking his turn.

"The honest answer is 'yes' and 'no.' If the hack is crude, the Bitcoin miners will raise a stink on the social media world—we should catch that. If she's slick, the first people to know will likely be looking at empty accounts totaling billions of dollars. They will react, but the question is how. If Putin is looking to create havoc in the inner circle, stealing the cash is a great place to start. The problem is that it could provoke a palace coup. He knows that, has said as much through his intermediary connection with Navalny. So, we suspect the approach is to create suspicions among a few oligarchs and let the circle fight it out. Some of those gentlemen employ what we could call a small army of former *Spetsnaz* and ex-military. None of whom travel light, if you know what I mean."

"A palace revolution where the only winner is Putin?" The DNI.

"Yes, in a very brutal manner. Putin cleans up the mess, announces his retirement, and lets Navalny win the election. And begins the cycle of recruiting a whole new group of loyalists. Shit, after twenty-six years atop that snake pit, I'd be looking to retire as well."

There was a pause. The implications of the Dog Pound work was now coming to the fore. We were predicting Russian succession with a hand on the potential champion's balls, ready to be squeezed when ordered. Washington hasn't had life that good since the banana republics threw us out.

"Problems we need to take into consideration?" The director. He was preparing for questions certain to be asked in the Oval.

"First, Fedor's no amateur. He shut down FSB, Moscow's equivalent of the FBI, and he's likely skated through all of Twitter, Instagram, and Facebook. For all I know he has thousands of accounts on those services. On a more interesting front, he operates a dark web sales site called Endless Horizons. Deals in everything from assassination to drugs and software access. All paid for in Bitcoin. Obviously maintains his own account somewhere online."

"We tried to get in?" The director again.

"Sir, I personally have worked that site and Fedor's servers. Pardon my French, but he's fucking good. That Fedor went in search of assistance suggests he's found someone who's even smarter. Our question, today, is who, and where she is. If she's in the U.S., we have the FBI on board. If she's offshore, it goes to Ops—that's why we're here."

Very quiet at the front of the room, the two politicos looked at each other.

I spoke the words they didn't want to utter. "We either turn this off digitally, or a couple people die. Either solution works for me. And, more importantly, for American national interests."

The DNI turned to his supposed subordinate—the director of CIA—subtly slumped in his suit and muttered one comment: "This one is all yours."

The Dog Pound was no longer on anyone's leash.

Except mine.

chapter

14

you can't fence everything in moscow, russia, 1 october 2025

Fedor was not a man of the calendar or clock. Every day was Monday and happy hour occurred when he logged off. Dr. Bakshi assured him all was well. In her normal cryptic email contact via that simple trick no one realized was resident until David Petraeus fucked it up, all for an affair with some floozy who would be lost to history. People recall famous men who drop their pants in the wrong bedroom. They seldom recall who was on the reciprocal side of that relationship.

Unless you were Monica Lewinsky or Fanne Foxe. Come on, you have to recall Fanne Foxe. A local stripper who was doing Congressman Wilbur Mills. When they were pulled over driving about Washington, DC, at 0200 after more than a few drinks, Fanne tried to escape attention by jumping into the Tidal Pool. Great headlines, and an even better scandal than Clinton-Lewinsky. Wilbur had to resign from Congress. Clinton hung on for a full eight years in the White House, despite being impeached.

But try coming up with other mistresses who survived the passage of time. Yes, yes, the rumors of Kennedy and Marilyn Monroe. That one survived as lore. But where was the evidence? No semen-stained dress. No reports of JFK sleeping on the couch—unlike Clinton. Shit, even Trump managed to dodge the bullet on god knows how many dalliances.

Back on track.

Fedor and Bakshi communicated in single, dual, sometimes triple-word sentences, by saving a draft email on an account they both could access. Oldest trick in the modern book of cyber covert communication. They'd both decided it was such a well-known ploy no one would go hunting down that path. They were right. Seemed too obvious for NSA to expend the time necessary to peel apart the billions of email accounts now in circulation.

Bakshi had started the conversation.

"Need help."

He'd responded. "What."

"Bots." Her retained draft email, left for him a day later.

"OK." That's all he wrote. They both knew he was considered a master of the bot kingdom.

"Meet." She'd posted that 24 September.

"I'll call you." His answer.

Nothing was going to happen until he met with Navalny. A feat of some intellectual effort.

First, he had to find the code word for October 2025. Just happened to be: "Available." At the outset of their partnership, Navalny had handed him a pocket calendar with a single word scribbled across the top of each month. The clues didn't end there. Fedor then needed to determine where the rendezvous would take place.

More deciphering of the mini-calendar. Navalny had selected each of the spots—without providing names—and then circled a date on the page for that month. This time the date was 10 October. Just to make life a little more complicated, the attorney chose to use the English alphabet. Twenty-six options, fit every month of the year. Unlike the thirty-three characters that make up the Russian Cyrillic alphabet, not many months with thirty-three days.

Pain in the ass as far as Fedor was concerned. Dredged up a set of the English alphabet in proper order on the internet, then picked the tenth letter, followed by a trip to the web to find a café with a name that started with the selected letter. This month it was a "J." He plugged in options for the Arbat neighborhood and came up with "Jeffery's Coffee." About nine hundred meters from Navalny's office. No surprise there, the lawyer didn't like to be inconvenienced or walk far.

He dialed Navalny's office. Secretary answered. No attorney picks up a phone if there's an assistant to screen calls. "Need to speak with Alexei." He was abrupt, hated the whole idea of this fuddling through a flunky before arriving at the "big man's" desk.

"Hold please."

She knew who it was. Registered the time and date in her memory. Her CIA handler wanted this data.

"Sir, call for you." She just yelled out the request for his attention. Shit, with an office this small there was no need for an intercom. Plus, she'd heard intercoms could be intercepted by listening devices. Given her bit of traitorous behavior, you never knew who could be listening in.

He picked up.

One word, "Available." That's all that was said.

Click.

Navalny looked at the clock. It was now 1030. That meant he had thirty minutes to wander over to Jeffery's. He finished reading a paper one of his research aides was preparing and reached for a jacket. Even at the beginning of October the temperature hovered at 40 degrees Fahrenheit. That, and rain was almost guaranteed. No need to rush, Fedor would be late. He always was.

Jeffery's is a funky place parked at 45 Starokonyushennyy Pereulok. It's a bit like going to a friend's kitchen or ramshackle living room for coffee and a snack. The advantage of Jeffery's is that they always have music playing in the background and you can see everyone coming and going. Made for an ideal spot to have a confidential conversation. The down side was that occasionally Navalny would find himself signing autographs for admiring twenty-somethings. The price of being a politician who wasn't universally loathed.

As expected, the computer wizard arrived twenty minutes after their agreed meeting time.

"You don't own a watch?" Navalny's sarcastic observation.

"Busy." Fedor was in monosyllabic mode. Navalny had seen this before. An apparent consequence of spending too much time engaged in conversations with only a computer or oneself. The lawyer suspected it was a bit of both.

"She wants to meet. In person." Fedor fended off the café staff, he'd had enough coffee. At this point in his day, a time period that began somewhere about 2230 the previous evening, he was ready for a drink. A beer or vodka would be good. That, and he was discouraged by the number of no smoking signs posted about the café. Who goes to drink coffee without a cigarette? At this pace Russia would no longer be Russia. He kept those thoughts to himself.

"Why?" Navalny was genuinely curious.

"Wants help."

"Thought you recruited her because she didn't need assistance." An attorney firing back at his client.

"This is a lot harder than you think." Fedor was on the verge of going back to explaining how to make the clock. Stopped himself.

"How far along do you think she is?" Fair question from a man now answering questions at the Kremlin and queries from Langley.

"Damn close." Fedor had lit a cigarette and ordered a beer. Fuck them, he was still in Russia—you want clean living, move to Europe or the United States. Wait, the Europeans still smoked and drank at noon. Go to the fucking U.S. The staff glared, he ignored the lot. A bunch of "kids" who likely could not spell "computer," less pull off what he was about to accomplish. An end to Putin, imagine.

Navalny sat and thought for a minute. "Where can you meet outside Russia—where neither of you will be arrested?"

"I thought about that." Fedor was feeling better; the beer or nicotine helped, maybe it was both. "I'm thinking Budapest. Government has proven unwilling to cooperate with EU laws, won't extradite to the West, and pays little attention to tourists—so long as they bring money."

For a computer geek, Navalny realized, the man did keep track of politics. The Hungarians had been the first EU member to essentially declare an end to liberal democracy. Victor Orban, the sitting prime minister since May 2010, was sixty-two, in reasonable health, and showed no interest in passing the scepter. In fact, he very much resembled, at least in the way Hungary was governed, Vladimir Putin. Budapest would be ideal. Large airport, population of two million and little interest in human rights or Russian business.

"When?" Obvious next question.

"Two days, maybe three." Fedor took a long drag on his cigarette and then vented in a manner directly intended to infuriate the staff.

"Why ask me? Sounds like you have a schedule in hand." Perhaps a bit too curt, Navalny realized that type of response might suggest to Fedor there was *indeed* a boss sitting across the table.

"Because, you have the most to lose if this goes wrong." Honest response, at least as best Fedor knew.

The man who would be king sat back in his chair. Carefully lifted a cup of tea to his lips and then reached for the obligatory snack basket placed on their table. Took a bite of a cookie, another sip of tea. And then set both items down on the table and leaned forward. Until his head and shoulders were a good quarter way across the small surface.

"Don't ask me how to shoot a man when you've already been given the order to commit an execution. You know what we want to accomplish. If it requires a trip to Budapest, take the fucking trip to Budapest." That came out as a snarl. "And don't call me for a meeting on such trivial shit ever again. Do what you have to do and then tell me why I should be worried."

Fedor just stared him in the eyes. There was no blink, no twitch, and certainly no nervous laugh. He'd been at the dark side of the computer world too long to be intimidated by a politician he was certain could be charred into electronic dust with little more than a few hours of typing and inventive thinking.

That was the moment Navalny realized he'd stepped into a trap of his own making.

What Putin could bless, Fedor might be well able to undo.

"I came to you with a respectable objective. Now you turn on me." Fedor was not asking or whining. He already knew Navalny was a man of ambition. It now dawned on him those ambitions might be more absolute than Fedor had initially expected.

"Bullshit, you came to me with an intent of toppling a government. Now you're asking permission?" Navalny shot back, still leaning across the table. Didn't even blink when Fedor exhaled a lungful of smoke into his face. "Children ask permission. Adults commit and beg forgiveness later." A pause. "You need to go to Budapest, go. Then complete the job. We're running out of time."

With that the attorney resumed a relaxed position. Another bite from the cookie and a sip of tea.

Fedor lit his second cigarette and took a few more swigs from the beer bottle. He was tired, too tired for this bullshit. Suddenly, sleep called.

"I'm done," he announced to Navalny. "I presume you bless whatever path we take to accomplish this task." The politician was not the only one who could ask rhetorical questions that required no answer.

Silence from the other side of the table, just a head nod indicating agreement.

Fedor abruptly stood, grabbed his jacket, and walked out. Beer half finished, a newly lit cigarette perched on the saucer for Navalny's tea cup.

Fuck, what had he done? There was a creeping shadow of doubt, perhaps fear, crawling over his consciousness. He'd long known Fedor was utterly without morals, but what he'd not expected was the "spine" suddenly on exhibit. This was not the disheveled digital master he normally encountered. That person had suddenly evaporated and become something quite, dare he say, evil.

He finished the cup of tea, paid the bill, tipped far too well, and apologized for his colleague's "Russian behavior." Civilized Muscovites were expected to know better. Then it dawned on him. Fedor was not "civilized," at least in a manner comprehensible to an everyday pedestrian passing by on the now-wet streets. Fedor lived in his own jungle, complete with its own rules. Many of which did not recognize the perfunctory respect accorded innocent bystanders or accidental intruders.

Just for a moment, just one, he wondered at the menace unleashed. A slip in his personal mental armor.

The walk back to his office was brisk. Weather was changing. Wind had shifted from the northeast to directly from the north. That would bring more rain, and sleet. Shit, weather only a Russian could love. He bent his head to avoid the rain splashing on his face and quickened the pace.

It was time to make another phone call. And dispatch his secretary for one of her second's meetings.

The phone call came first. He walked into a convenience store two blocks from Jeffery's and purchased a burner. Another throwaway cell. Navalny occasionally wondered how many of these damn things had passed through his hands in the last fifteen years. One hundred, one hundred fifty? Didn't matter. What Putin's stooges failed to pay for the CIA covered.

He walked out, then dodged behind the corner of a building. Took him out of the wind and most of the rain. A single call, memorized number, two rings. Then the familiar answer, "Hello?"

"Checking in."

"Yes, I have you." CIA simply acknowledging they knew who was on the other end of this call.

"Boy Wonder is closer than believed. Headed for Budapest in the next two or three days. Set to meet with the other big dog." Then he hung up. Dropped the phone into a trashcan piled with lunch litter and a few beer bottles. No one was going to rummage through that debris.

Took him ten minutes to cover the remaining ground. Upon reaching the office he simply placed his hand on the secretary's shoulder. A sign they needed to go for a walk. In this case up to the roof, ostensibly to smoke. He'd forbidden smoking in the office, it offended visiting journalists. The excuse, they needed every ruble that sympathetic news coverage could draw. So, he and the secretary always trod up the stairs, three flights to the rooftop. There was a small sheltered area. He was not the only one to demand work spaces remain cigarette free.

She lit one, passed it to him. Lit another for herself. He'd quit years before, but to provide an excuse for these conversations Navalny was willing to violate the rules. His wife still smoked, which seemingly kept her from detecting this transgression. The secretary looked him in the eye, she was long past social niceties. This was a relationship that could, quite reasonably, result in one, or both, of them dead.

"Set up a meeting." His request.

"*Da*, what this time?"

"Fedor is coming. Soon. Our mutual friend should know that. I expect in less than a week."

She finished her cigarette. "You know what this means?"

"Yes, either you will get promoted or be sleeping with Rasputin." There was no humor in his voice, just a statement of fact.

"I prefer the promotion. Never liked unwashed Russian clerics." She walked back into the building.

He wondered what Fedor was doing.

Fedor, having climbed off the subway, made it to his apartment, let himself in, secured the locks, and set the alarm system, was sipping a final shot of vodka for this day. His draft email was simple. "Budapest, two days. Will call upon arrival." Saved the draft and logged off.

Figured she would not need to ask how he would know when she arrived or on what airline. That was child's play.

chapter 15

never promise there is a tomorrow

montgomery, alabama, 2 october 2025

Adya Bakshi detested Fedor Ivanov more than one could really appreciate. Had never met the man, had no idea what he looked like, and had no, zero, interest in spending time with him in Montgomery, let alone traveling for at least eightteen hours to meet with him in Budapest. She just could see no means of getting around this inconvenience without jeopardizing a venture that had now consumed more than a month of her life.

Somewhere in the back of her conscious there was a tingling that suggested others were watching and listening. And it was not just Fedor. The tingling was a familiar phenomenon. Likely a by-product of working on projects where the target was apt to be just as engaged in a counterintelligence campaign. She'd once pulled the team off a Facebook page production aimed at derailing a congressional campaign in California when the tingle turned into alarm bells.

Call it analyst intuition. The trap she left behind ensnared a Silicon Valley firm covertly hired to provide cyber security for the would-be congressman. Bakshi watched online as the "security specialist" wormed into her coding—only to discover he or she was caught in a bit of malware from which there was no extraction—save sending her a payment to unlock the computer they were working from. The ransom money was required to arrive in a stipulated forty-eight hour period. When they failed to comply she wiped the machine's hard drive and left a message on the screen saver. "We are watching."

The tingle now was worthy of her attention.

She just could not figure out who. The Chinese failed to capture her SCADA attack. Bakshi's presence in Russia was limited to the draft emails to Fedor. To this point there was no indication of domestic intrusion... NSA—the Snowden files left every hacker in America nervous. For all intents and purposes, she was a nonpresence. At least on the World Wide Web. And yet, the tingle continued. Bid her to take precautions, both digital and physical.

Rather than create a paper trail from Montgomery to Budapest, the good doctor opted to fly from Atlanta. Four options—every one of them demanded a stop. Pick your poison, Air France, Delta, KLM, or Lufthansa. Air France and Delta stopped in Paris. KLM routed her through Amsterdam. Lufthansa, predictably, demanded a plane change in Frankfurt. She went with Delta. Headquartered in Atlanta, Delta's operations in and out of that city were likely to be sufficient to bury her transactions in a sea of data.

Opted to fly economy class. Despite the discomfort and fact that she could afford to upgrade to business or even the vaunted front rows. Again, a bid to avoid drawing attention. Round trip cost $2,500. Set for 3 October to 8 October, a long weekend in Budapest. A well-deserved vacation, if anyone asked. Paid for it via Bitcoin. No one collected travel miles anymore. And she didn't want a record on her credit card.

Arranged for a rental car through Hertz. Did not want the miles on her vehicle. Scheduled a taxi to drop her off at the Hertz lot. All paid in Bitcoin. The goal was to leave as few trackable movements as possible. In a further bid to avoid suspicion she went so far as to call one of the business partners and request he move her car about the parking lot at the apartment complex, every other day for a week or until she called. "Just do it at night" was her sole instruction; that would leave the neighbors thinking she was still home and shuffling about—the "ghost" they were accustomed to not seeing, but knew resided in their midst.

Even those preparations failed to pacify the tingle.

Chose a set of clothes suitable for the weather, nothing flashy. Temperature in Budapest averaged about 45 degrees and it rained almost every other day. She went with jeans, a couple of shirts, a warm sweatshirt, and a waterproof jacket. All in dark colors. Pulled out an old black folding umbrella and a pair of slip-on loafers. On top of that were underwear and a set of pajamas. Minimal cosmetics and a few toiletries. All fit into the roll-on without a problem.

Debated over a briefcase with one of the laptops. Then opted out. The only electronic device on her person was a cell phone. The two USBs went into the toes of the loafers. Encrypted, of course, but still a vulnerability. There was simply no other means of transporting the coding and data she needed to discuss with Fedor.

Final bit of her "vacation" cover. A book for the airplane. Chose a classic—Neal Stephenson's *Cryptonomicon.* All too appropriate. An Indian woman with a background in IT reading a novel about establishing a "data haven" in Southeast Asia. One where encrypted data could be stored without fear of prying eyes or government intrusion. Yeah, right. She gave Stephenson a pass on the latter. He was writing back in the mid-1990s. The days of near universal "digital immigration." At 918 pages she figured the novel would keep her busy and prevent seatmates from pestering her with idle gossip or endless personal questions. To say nothing of the fact she would never have this much spare time on her hands again in the foreseeable future.

At the last minute she grabbed the iPod Shuffle—the sixth generation held three hundred songs, played for up to twenty-four hours without recharging, and, best of all, Bluetoothed to a set of headphones. Hers was loaded with traditional Arabic music. Dr. Bakshi had never developed a taste for Indian pop artists. Damn sure had no interest in listening to rock and roll or European classical schmaltz.

Put the iPod, book, and a light sweater into a small backpack.

Took a shower, dressed in a pair of black jeans, dark turtleneck, and a pair of sneakers. Not jogging shoes. Sneakers. Converse high tops. They were fashionable, in a computer geek sort of way, and had the advantage of being comfortable. Called a cab and started her way to Budapest. It was going to be a long, long day.

moscow, russia, 2 october 2025

Nice thing about living only two and a half flying hours from your destination. Last-minute preparation. Shit, it wasn't like Budapest was some remote outpost. If you forgot something, go to a store or request the hotel deliver the item in question. That was Fedor's complete list of thoughts on travel. Frankly, he hated to travel. Aside from wandering about Moscow. And even there he was best characterized as a homebody. The Mercedes—now nearly six years old—had fewer than twenty thousand kilometers under its wheels. Pain in the ass to park anywhere these days. Simpler to take the subway. Plus, Moscow's traffic was horrendous, even at midnight.

Perhaps it would be wisest to say traffic was at its worst come midnight. At least half the drivers were guaranteed to be drunk. Including the police. He stayed off the roads between midnight and six o'clock.

Fedor's fastidious personality quirks actually made the process of packing fairly straightforward. Clothing items of choice were either on hangers or in the drawers where they belonged. His roll-on, a brand-new Amazon delivery (yes, they have Amazon in Moscow), provided all the space he needed for a pair of faded jeans, a couple of dingy T-shirts, three pairs of underwear, and a shabby hoodie. All the clothing a hacker needed. Not like he was expecting to leave the hotel or play tourist.

Then the process became a bit more complicated. Like Bakshi, he'd downloaded everything required for this trip onto a pair of USB sticks. Those went into a concealed pocket of his battered leather satchel. Used to be a decent bag, almost worthy of being toted into a courtroom by some high-priced attorney.

No more. Over the course of ten years he'd "weathered" the satchel. And worn it in. The once stiff leather sides sagged, the bright brown finish was now a scratched and gray façade. And then he'd taken it to a specialty shop and had them work on his abuse. As in "make it worse." At the same time, he demanded reinforced corners be sewn in the satchel so as to disguise the presence of an iPod or USB. In order to prevent airport security or anyone else with an X-ray machine discovering what he was carrying. Worked like a charm.

To complete the disheveled appearance of his work bag, he would always add a stack of random printouts, old newspapers and, typically, a half-crushed sandwich wrapped in cellophane next to an obviously abused bag of potato chips. Never carry fruit. Such an act of healthiness made you a suspicious character in Russian airports. Better to have a couple of packs of cigarettes jammed atop the sandwich and chips.

He was never searched at a Russian airport. Didn't hurt that he also arrived reeking of yesterday night's vodka binge. That usually meant a few shots just before he climbed into a taxi to catch the flight, but since he hated flying anyway, why be sober?

The grand debate had come down to whether he should take a laptop—there were a couple in the apartment completely void of data—they were his "zombies," machines that could be used to access the web anywhere without fear of adverse consequences should he be arrested, or the machine stolen. He ran generic software on both zombies. No sign of his coding skills or a potential indication as to the presence of Endless Horizons. In the end he opted out of carrying one with him. There was already enough paranoia about Russian hacking in eastern Europe. He stuck with an ancient Android cell phone.

Made reservations on the Aeroflot direct flight to Budapest. Then went in search of a hotel with two rooms that would not draw suspicion. Chose to book with the InterContinental Budapest. Reserved two deluxe rooms overlooking the Danube River and famous

Chain Bridge. Came with a separate check-in area, valet service, and high-speed internet. He might desire the former two options, the third was a must. Made sure they were booked for anything above the fourth floor. No prying eyes or listening gear trained on the windows.

Paid in advance. Bitcoin. Hotel rooms were in her name. He planned to leave as small a footprint as possible.

Then it was time to go shopping. Found Compker, located on Visegrádi street. Short taxi ride from the hotel. Had everything he needed. A pair of serious laptops and a printer for reasonable prices. Placed an order and requested they be loaded with the latest Microsoft office suite and stripped of anything Kaspersky. One of the USBs in his satchel had all the firewall security they might require.

With that he went into a search mode. Betting Bakshi made her reservations under her real identity. Nice thing about airline databases; little effort to impose security—think Expedia, KAYAK, and Travelocity. Those online travel sites ensured the boys and girls charged with maintaining reservations access kept the firewalls at a bare minimum. Drove the cyber security gurus nuts. Made his life a lot simpler.

Took an educated guess, figured she wasn't so foolish as to fly out of Montgomery. Place was a fly speck on the global map. A passenger booking round trip from there to Budapest was going to catch the attention of America's Homeland Security. So where next? He'd pulled up the airline schedules. Easiest route was Atlanta. OK, start his dredging from there.

Took all of five minutes. Doesn't hurt when you're hunting for "Adya Bakshi." Would have been more work finding Frank Brown or, god forbid, Susan Smith. Bakshi was easy. He jotted down her arrival time, noted it was Delta, and climbed online. Quick stop at Blacklane, they were global these days. Requested a BMW 5-series and a driver with a placard to be standing by the customs clearance portal. Also provided drop-off instructions. Again, advance pay in Bitcoin. Oh, he'd requested the Mercedes S-class service for himself. No reason to be uncomfortable.

The skinny Indian woman could squeeze into the Beemer. He planned on a vehicle that came with a broad backseat and a couple of bottles stuck in the armrest that separated the backseat occupants.

The least pleasant bit of his preparations. Reservations at the last minute on Aeroflot. FSB kept its thumb pressed on the Aeroflot reservations staff. Just like the Americans, they had a no-fly list. Mostly Chechens, but there were a few criminals, cyber-types, and politicians who were strictly prohibited from leaving the country. Travel where you like within Mother Russia. Attempt to *leave* the country... well.

Fedor had tried repeatedly to access that database. To no avail. The damn Russian government purchased software from the Americans, who'd spent a fortune on continuous upgrades to "protect the innocent" and avoid alerting the guilty. Fuck.

He took his chances. Processed the ticket order and paid, again, in Bitcoin. Then waited. Sweating. Here was where the whole train could go off the rails.

Took almost eight minutes for the reservation to go through. He wrote that off to crappy software and old equipment. This was Aeroflot, after all. Interestingly, the Bitcoin transaction went through in less than two minutes. A lot faster than he'd encountered at the last three of his purchases. Funny, in an ironic way, that Aeroflot is processing payments more expeditiously than InterContinental. Must be a glitch in the Hungarian internet services.

His only thought.

Sloppy thinking. Perhaps it was the vodka from this "morning's" breakfast. He'd awakened at 1300. Early for him. Still hungover from the night before, had opted for hair of the dog. Seemed wise at the time. Should have thought twice. While Putin could protect him from the FSB, there was nothing the Russian leader could do to halt Washington's interest in Fedor.

The delay in the transaction was not Aeroflot. It was the international no-fly database connecting to servers across the planet.

washington, dc, 2 october 2025

I'm always up at 0500. Never in the best mood. Fucking coffee machine takes its own sweet time to generate a cup of liquid caffeine. Trust me, baby, I don't waste time on that drip or percolator shit. I have a Breville espresso maker. But still, fucking $500 machine takes its own damn time before coming to life. Gives me a couple of minutes to grind fresh beans. Keep them in a sealed container—on the counter. That story about coffee stays freshest when frozen; misleading wives' tale. Freezer dries the beans out. Less humidity in the freezer. If it makes you feel better to keep them cold, stick the container in your refrigerator.

So here it is, 0500. My hair is a mess, Wiper wants out to pee, and the Breville is just thinking about getting up to speed. The only thing I've managed to do is grind the beans, fill the filter cup, clamp it back in. Don't have that much common sense at this time of day.

Damn phone starts ringing. No caller ID available. Fuck, I *know* who this is.

"Veterinarian here." That's all I say to these clowns. It's my 24/7 watch team.

"Boy Wonder just booked a flight to Budapest." Nothing else said. No need. I knew what they were telling me.

"When."

"Today, last flight of the schedule, 2135 Moscow time."

Like I think in Moscow time at 0500 in Washington, DC. Going to fire one of these watch standers to make an example of the cost of idiocy.

Guess they were reading my mind.

"That would be 1235 here."

"Got it, alert Ops. I'll be in at 0900. Need to make another phone call. Then hit the gym."

No comment about the gym appointment; they knew better. Let Wiper out to pollute flowers and fertilize the backyard. Remembered to stick a coffee cup under the filter drip. Picked up the phone and dialed.

Now you get to learn what my brother *really* does for a living.

chapter 16

setting loose the dog catcher

washington, dc, 2 october 2025

Yes, yes, I've been promising to tell you about my brother for weeks. You remember, the boy who went to the Naval Academy and then joined the Marine Corps. Dumb ass, even I know the Air Force has better golf courses. The brother who went to Iraq twice and Afghanistan four times. Married a white girl, lives down the street from me, two kids. I know I told you all this shit before.

Well, baby brother never wanted to tell me how he was paying the bills aside from the Marine Corps reserve gig. Trust me, no one pays for a house on Capitol Hill by serving as a weekend warrior. And his wife's job as some Greenpeace wacko at a nonprofit sure ain't covering the mortgage. Told you all this before as well. Damn, you people do *not* listen.

Here's what baby brother told me: He was a contractor for the DC police department. Ran down hard cases. Bullshit. The man's six foot four, weighs in at 220, and benches a little over double that. Chases me around the gym in the morning when it appears I'm slacking. At that size and with his Marine Corps bearing—that's "posture" to the uninitiated—he doesn't just slink into backrooms and dusty archives. Probably would be less obvious if he'd grown some hair on his dome, but he insists on the shaved look. Claims his wife finds it sexy. Whatever.

Whole charade made me suspicious, so I went and broke the rules. No, I broke the law—the intelligence community isn't supposed to be spying on American citizens. Not, at least, without a court order. Screw the attorneys. Shakespeare was right. "The first thing we do, let's kill all the lawyers." I'm not kidding, Read *Henry VI,* it's in Part 2, Act IV, Scene 2. What? Surprised I read just because I'm a computer nerd? Took all the humanities classes in college and two semesters of Shakespeare.

Here's what I learned. First, my brother and his wife have the most boring email exchanges you can possibly imagine... all about groceries and who is picking up or dropping off the kids. Sure as hell ain't sexting. Someone shoot me when I reach that level of mundane in a relationship.

Second, the son of a bitch—pardon me, Momma, if you're reading this, it's just an expression of speech, not intended as an insult—works for my employer. Completely undercover. Different name, the whole game. Hell, *I* wouldn't recognize his passport picture nor be able to find any record of his other persona.

Cute. In an unfunny sort of way. He *knew* where I worked. He might have told me.

Turnabout is fair play. That second call, the one that took place at 0511 on 2 October. That went to the Ops control desk. Same kids that Navalny calls. Here's how it went.

"Tell 'Darnell Johnston' his black ass better be in the Ops conference room at 0900 this morning." Crappy cover name for a boy my mother proudly named Booker, as in Booker T. Washington. Go look him up. Born a slave and ended up founding the Tuskegee Institute, among other things. If Momma knew my brother was going by "Darnell," there'd be hell to pay.

Finally got Wiper back in the house, pulled on my gym stuff, and drove over to Results. Usual crowd, including Darnell who gave me a funny look on his way to the third-floor weight room. Yoga day for me. Thursday class is run by some cranky old white woman who can fold herself into a pretzel. I'm telling you, that woman is at least seventy and puts to shame both men and women forty years younger. And she has no sympathy for my act. I get the nasty comments and physical corrections as frequently as everyone else in the room.

Let me tell you, yoga ain't for sissies. At least not the way this woman teaches it.

An hour of that, a quick dash through the weight machines, and I hit the shower. Still needed my bagel and another shot of espresso before heading to Langley. Knowing the Dog Pound team, they're back to eating day-old doughnuts and drinking burned coffee. If the scientists are right, that crap will kill them long before I'll get the chance. Rather have the good stuff out of my own pantry.

Manage to merge onto the I-395 viaduct at 0815. It was a grab-and-dash breakfast. Usual nasty traffic. But with any luck, I'd be right on the edge of 0900 when rolling in. The Tesla takes no prisoners.

Spent the entire drive wondering if Darnell would be equally punctual. Let me fill you in on an old, not-so-secret joke shared within the African-American community. It's called CPT. Colored People's Time. No white boy came up with that. It's a poke at ourselves. Because it seems like no African-American can make it to a social function less than fifteen to twenty minutes late.

This was no social gathering. He'd be there on the mark. I know my brother. The Naval Academy and Marine Corps beat punctuality into his soul. He's done the same to his kids. His wife, on the other hand, is on WPT. That'd be White People's Time. Where you show up to everything five minutes late to demonstrate just how "busy" or "important" you are. Almost as annoying as CPT, except white people think they can get away with this everywhere. Including church.

We are going to ruin as a civilization.

Actually, we were well on our way to ruin long before 2025. I might argue somewhere about 1968, but that's just my opinion. You can have your own.

Rolled in the doors at 0855. Looked around the room. Usual suspects, including my elderly Russian specialist. He looked older by the day. Didn't help we had him on a short leash. That meant taking home a secure phone and being on call around the clock. The watch teams were milking every insight they could get from that poor bastard. The price of selling your soul to peddle opinions. Or was that "wisdom"? Everyone needs their fifteen minutes of fame. This was his.

Darnell strode in with the Ops director at 0900 on the mark. No CPT here. I gave my brother the snake eye. He ignored me. The Ops director just provided a knowing smile. He figured this was a twist not inked on my white board. I hate fucking surprises. Particularly when they involve close relatives.

The big boss gave me a quick glance, then opened the session with a no-shit question.

Bastard, he was the one who demanded we provide continual updates. My apologies for interrupting your day, perhaps you forgot this is *your job.* Honestly, where do they find these people? And then promote them? Get over yourself, the rest of us have more than an 80 IQ as well.

"Sir, Fedor is headed to Budapest, will be there in the next three hours. Comms intercepts indicate he's going to meet with his U.S. counterpart. Way ahead of what we understood as a 1 November timeline." My opening shot.

"And . . ." The Ops chief waiting for tasking.

Never, ever call in the boss unless you have a plan for him to haul up the chain of command.

"Our analysts are convinced, or at least have the evidence to suggest, Fedor never leaves Russia. This must be important." I left off the action step I was about to request. Best to let the sexy shit soak in before going for the jugular.

"Confirmation?" The boss man knew how to fire back.

"Navalny called in." That's all I needed to say. In a split second it went from confrontation to affirmative collaboration.

"Which explains your explicit request for Darnell." The boss is now on my brainwave. Got to love when that happens.

"Sir, Darnell has the skills necessary to make Fedor ours." A politically correct means of requesting a "rendition." Fancy way of saying we go in and kidnap the suspect, then park him or her someplace unpleasant for a bit of "questioning." Hey, I don't give a shit what the FBI thinks, everything I've seen leaves the impression waterboarding really works. A lot more graceful than yanking fingernails or employing a blowtorch.

Problem with those other methods, they leave a trail of physical evidence. Waterboarding has no such downside, unless the interrogating party is stupid enough to record the event. CIA didn't put cameras into the black site interrogation rooms anymore. At best there was an audio recording. But even that was rare. Standard procedure was to trust the persons conducting an "interview." Not like we were planning to use the information as evidence in a courtroom anyway. Just to intercept bad guys and determine who needed a visit from one of our drones next.

Following me?

We know Fedor never bothers with a gym. You can bet he has no idea how to swim. Waterboarding works best on people afraid of drowning. How many Middle Easterners or Afghanis have you met at the swimming pool? That's why CIA went to the waterboard. Works best on people whose familiarity with the liquid stuff is limited to a bathtub or shower. Fedor was one of those.

So here I was, bluntly requesting Fedor go for a longer trip than the Russian hacker expected. With a "spa treatment" that would likely help with his weight problem, but do nothing for his complexion. I bet his plants in that fancy apartment will be dead by the time he gets back. Hope he doesn't have a cat or a fish tank.

This is what my brother does. Very effectively.

There was my plan. Now I was waiting for an answer from the Ops director in a room filled with people who'd been working this problem nonstop for more than a month.

He glanced around. "What do you want from Fedor?" His next question.

"How, who he's working with, and what he targets. We don't want him burning one of our assets." Thought that was a reasonable response.

"If he doesn't cooperate?" The boss was no fool. Some idiots would rather die than betray.

"Fedor is not that brave, he is not his father." My elderly Russian analyst chiming in. "He'll talk, and then demand asylum. Will not be able to go back to Russia."

"Shit, that's just what we need, another Russian exile on the U.S. payroll." The Ops director forgot who he was talking to, or perhaps didn't know, I couldn't tell. But it was the wrong thing to say.

From the back of the room my indispensable analyst fired back. "And without us you would still be dealing with the USSR. 'Pick your drink,' as we say in Russia, 'but it will always be vodka. The other options are unacceptable substitutes.'"

Touché, I had to give the old man credit.

"If I say no?" Man didn't become the director of Operations at CIA by accident. There was more than a little political and professional moxie involved.

My turn. "We live with the consequences, potentially lose Navalny, and have at least two cyber wizards running free. One of whom has obvious access to live and operate in this country."

That caused things to go silent in the room. Darnell just shot me a look. I could read that glance, it meant, "Girl, you got *cojones*."

"So how do we find Fedor? Budapest is not some backwoods village in Afghanistan, Iraq, Syria, or any other third-world shithole you can name." The boss man was throwing down his gauntlet.

That's when my ace-in-the-hole stepped in. Should say stood up. The old Russian bastard actually got out of his chair.

"Fedor is spoiled, he will not stay in any cheap hotel. He will not operate without high-speed internet access, and he will want to be positioned for a return to Russia with the least attention possible. Add to that he will have requested two hotel rooms, likely adjoining to avoid time spent in public spaces. I suspect…" Here the old man cleared his throat—smoking was going to kill him sooner or later, I hoped later. "I suspect," he continued, "he will also seek a place with easy access to computer equipment. Fedor is not so stupid as to travel out of Russia with his own gear."

My new superstar sat down. Out of breath.

"Reasonable assumptions." The boss was back to being the boss. "Anyone have a list of likely hotels?"

"Working on it." That was my rep from NGA. Those imagery guys also worked mapping. They knew more about Budapest than most locals. And had been smart enough to start coordinating with the other team members as soon as news of Fedor's trip reached the Dog Pound.

A bitter retort from the boss. "I'm about to send a man to Hungary in search of a single Russian hacker and we're still 'working' on it? Young man, have you ever been to Budapest?"

That was uncalled for, a direct insult. I could have bitch-slapped the man right there. No reason to go all "senior" on people working their asses off.

I should stop underestimating the millennials. Kid fired back with both barrels. "If your team can punch out a list of the most likely hotels in the next two hours, we're all ears. Hell, I'd be happy to go home and see my wife and kids while your experts handle the whole affair. It only took them ten years to find Bin Laden, and he was parked with one of your close allies. I don't think Fedor's going to build a villa and stay put for half a decade."

Ouch.

"Gentlemen," I intruded, before the verbal bloodshed began, "we obviously need a few more hours to compile the likely hotels. Meanwhile, Darnell there best get his ass on an airplane." I fired Darnell a "you better be moving, asshole" look.

The Ops director took the clue. No sense in turning this into an interagency slugfest, which it always becomes in the Beltway bureaucracy. My bet, he already knew the young man was preparing to call back to mother NGA and then start a manager-to-manager bicker.

I sure as shit didn't need that crap now.

Meeting over, the Ops boss walked out. I knew how to read that. Act now, before there were second thoughts.

"Darnell." I'd rolled up to my standing brother. "You better be on the next flight to Budapest, need me to make your ass a reservation? Oh, don't forget to remind your kids my Wiper still requires two walks a day before you get on that airplane."

He smiled at me, in a pained sort of way, left without comment.

See, I told you my brother had an interesting job. Now we'll find out if Booker's earning that government salary he "forgot" to tell me about for the last three years.

chapter

17

standing on the precipice
budapest, hungary, 3 october 2025

Regardless of the hours one chooses to operate or sleep, jet lag is jet lag. Dr. Bakshi was suffering a nasty case of it by the time she spotted the driver in Budapest's airport. Didn't help that it was 0930 Budapest time or that her scheduled Delta flight turned out to be Air France and routed through Paris—she hated Charles de Gaulle Airport. Place was a damned puzzle palace. Essentially a day of her life lost in transit. And the whole charade would have to be repeated in less than a week. Why, she wondered, do people do this to themselves? And pay for it?

The waiting automobile was a nice touch. To be honest, she expected nothing less than curbside service. Nor had any delusion that Fedor would serve as the chauffeur. All the better; she needed a bit of alone time to decompress from the "cattle car" experience of flying in economy class. The BMW was perfect. Heated rear seat, a silent driver, and a smooth ride.

She didn't bother to ask about cost. Presumed it was paid in advance. Did offer the man a twenty-dollar bill when they arrived at what she assumed was her hotel. He declined. In strained English simply declared, "It is already done." He was kind enough to retrieve her roll-on from the trunk and then was gone. Acted as though he had a busy schedule.

She walked into the lobby and was immediately greeted by a concierge. He requested her name, checked a list on a clipboard that obviously never left his side, and immediately escorted Bakshi to an inconspicuous check-in counter away from the normal lobby traffic.

"I believe I have a room for one reserved." Her comment to the young lady sitting behind the marble-topped counter.

The response was a little surprising. "Ms. Bakshi, we have you on the schedule for two rooms. Your traveling companion has already checked in. You will find him in the room immediately to the left of yours, number 612." All said in a faultless British accent. "Here is your keycard. Please do not hesitate to contact guest services should you require anything. Welcome to the InterContinental."

No further chitchat from the clerk. Bakshi reached for the handle on her suitcase and walked through the lobby to the lifts, dragging the bag behind on its wheels. She only called them elevators when dealing with people who could be presumed unfamiliar with the old-fashioned terminology. All Indian children who went to proper schools would refer to those infernal boxes as "lifts." Just could not presume, however, that a Hungarian would have received the same education. Must be the jet lag, she was feeling haughty. You can take the girl from the caste, but you cannot take the caste consciousness from the girl.

Selected the sixth floor. Noticed even the elevator had a marble floor. Walked out and turned left, room 610. She had no interest in encountering Fedor before a shower and a cup of tea. Keycard worked without hesitation. She dumped the suitcase on the king-sized bed and dialed room service.

"Oolong tea and plate of fruit." No please or thank you. Nor a consideration for cost. If Fedor could afford this place, he could pay for tea and a morning meal. As far as she was concerned, he was going to pay for more than that.

In room 612, Fedor heard the door slam shut on 610. Had to be Bakshi; the hotel operated under a strict no early check-in policy. He'd been compelled to reserve the room for her a day before the flight's arrival. The last thing he wanted to deal with was a grumpy, jet-lagged Indian woman. Not that he knew anything about Indian women. Or women in general.

Fedor had been busy. Spent much of the last ten hours setting up the two new laptops and then configuring access to Endless Horizons so he could continue earning a living while sitting in some damn hotel. He would be the first to admit the service was good. Somewhere around 0300 he'd gotten the urge for both coffee and vodka—"Russian breakfast." Delivery happened in less than fifteen minutes. Better than home. Fedor was a kitchen klutz. Even the coffeemaker succeeded in defeating him on bad days.

At this point both machines were loaded with Microsoft Office. In addition, they were running Adobe Acrobat Distiller DC and operating behind his personally designed firewall. He'd also installed a bit of software called Game Over. Was an option permanently displayed on the toolbar at the bottom of a standard Windows 12 display screen. Push that app once and the entire hard drive wiped itself. And then permanently parked itself. No smoke or noise, just a quiet, effective, electronic demise. All in less than 120 seconds.

Typical hotel, he could hear when the shower in her room turned on and then, five minutes later, off. Figured it would take another thirty minutes for her to get dressed and put on makeup.

Bakshi knocked on his door exactly ten minutes after turning the shower off. She never saw the purpose in diddling around with eye shadow or fussing with her hair. Just pulled it back into a ponytail and found a clean pair of jeans with a fresh blouse. Then she grabbed the sweatshirt and yanked that over her top. Good enough.

Strange. For the last day the tingle was gone. Disappeared when she climbed into the rental car and headed for Atlanta. Bakshi had suspected that, if anything, it would get worse the closer she approached this meeting with Fedor. The opposite was true.

He was everything she expected when the door opened. A chubby, disheveled Russian man smoking a cigarette and reeking of alcohol. The stack of room service dishes he'd forgotten to set outside in the hallway for pickup and the unmade bed further confirmed her suspicions. Uncouth drunken slob.

What did surprise her were the pair of laptops running on a hotel desk that Fedor had dragged to face out over a spectacular view of the Hungarian Parliament Building. That, and the fact he'd obviously connected them with the latest HP printer. The man had been busy, despite his wayward appearance.

"Doctor." His bid at a bit of professionalism. "You requested this meeting, you begin."

Silence, nothing but silence, for a full ninety seconds. How to explain what was coming? She spoke.

"I am ready to execute, but require assistance with one more step."

He said nothing, just reached for a coffee cup that obviously was serving as more of a shot glass than a container for caffeine. Took a sip, put it back on the desk. "I'm listening."

"We need a phishing campaign that will insert the transaction requests I've written. It needs to be coded so that as soon as we have all thirty-five of the transactions go live I am alerted and can immediately set off the required second step."

"Which is? Where is the money going?"

He surprised her with that second question. To that point there had been an internal philosophical debate between her ears. One side contended it could be dumped into accounts that she could access to benefit friends and family. A second put forth the idea of "vaporizing" the funds. Lose them forever in the bits and bytes of the digital universe. The third had been pushing the lot into the Gates Foundation under the guise of an anonymous donor. With a requirement it be used for alleviating poverty in India and Africa. She'd selected option one. If you decide to abet the deaths of three thousand people, why suddenly become a philanthropist?

"I haven't decided." Her uncommitted response to his query. "You have a preference?"

"Yes, we feed the money into Navalny's political operations. Just one more step in ridding Russia of Putin."

Bakshi said nothing. They both knew what she was thinking. The transactions could flow that surplus in multiple directions and no one would be the wiser. A billion to Navalny, a billion to her accounts, a billion to Gates... by her estimates that still left more than $5 or $6 billion to selectively distribute. She just nodded an affirmative in Fedor's direction.

"How long will it take you to craft the bot delivery and push it out?" Her verbal inquiry.

"You have addresses?" His pushback.

Indeed, she did. The last month had not just been expended on figuring out how to crack blockchain and SCADA. One of her laptops had been set up with an algorithm that did nothing but hunt Bitcoin miners. She'd done it right, a bit of AI coding. Once the machine discerned the online behaviors of one, two, three, ten, fifty Bitcoin miners it became ever more adept at identifying the next one hundred, one thousand, ten thousand. She had email addresses and URLs for almost every one of them. All on that second USB stuck in a loafer tucked away just one door's distance from where they sat. She nodded.

"Give me four, five hours and then bring the data." Fedor issuing orders. "Take one of the machines with you. It would be a good idea to monitor blockchain activity. I'm worried someone is watching. Someone who does not want us to know they are here... How do you say in English? 'Looking over my shoulder.'" Fedor sounding the alarm bell.

She lost her patience at that point. Blame the stress and weariness associated with travel. "Why the hell do you think I would fly across the planet to see *you*?" She spit out the last word of that rhetorical statement. "I *am sure* someone is tracking this 'fun and games' you've trapped me in. I just don't know who ... yet."

With that Bakshi stood, closed the top on one of the laptops—a random choice, she suspected both were set up with keystroke monitoring software—pulled the power cord out of the wall for her selected box, and walked out of the room.

Let the door slam behind her. When she left his room and then when she entered 610.

The tingling was back.

washington, dc, 3 october 2025

Back at headquarters, again. This commuting thing is getting damn old. No boss man in the workspaces this time, just the analysts and law enforcement. Oh, and Darnell. Time we get him up to speed. It's 0530, not my idea of the best moment to gather brain cells. To say nothing of that gym addiction. But they've got two gyms out here, so once we're done, I'll grab my bag of gear and head down to the "hallowed spaces."

Pissed off the IT gurus yesterday. Demanded they hang up another display screen and projector and install all the connections—in six hours. Lots of bitching and moaning. Finally got sick of their shit and called the Ops director's office. A little firepower from above cured the bad attitudes. And we are now as slick as CNN. I want to be able to do split screen in 6 x 8. That's six feet tall by eight feet wide. Baby, this morning, I can do that.

Just an observation between us. Now, I like my NGA guys, but they ain't NPIC. Let me explain. Back in the day, CIA ran its own set of imagery gurus, called them the National Photographic Interpretation Center. But also back then, the boys and girls employed at something called the National Imagery and Mapping Agency worked for DoD—that funny five-sided building. Well, the NIMA kids referred to their counterparts at CIA as the "NPIC Cowboys." Supposedly the NPIC kids ran through imagery faster and made calls quicker than the DoD bureaucrats liked. Fact of the matter, DoD was slow. NPIC kept beating them to the line. So, the fucking bureaucrats figured out how to kill NPIC.

Assholes.

I miss my NPIC Cowboys, particularly when we're under this kind of pressure.

But, bless their little hearts, NGA has decided to deliver. So Darnell can go shopping. In no particular order, mind you. Prestige Hotel Budapest, Danubius Hotel City Center, Eurostars Budapest Center, Hotel Parlament, Mercure Budapest Center, InterContinental Budapest, Budapest Marriott Hotel, and Starlight Suiten Hotel Budapest.

Great, but keep in mind there are over 4,700 hotels in Budapest. So, before I go rip a new asshole in one of the NGA guys who dragged me in here at 0400, might be best to listen. Turns out they took to heart the advice from our old Russian guru. That makes life a little easier for Darnell. That and the fact the NSA types pushed out a quick burn on Fedor's last phone call (we know now approximately when he left Moscow) and then picked up his first attempt to connect with email via a cell phone upon landing in Budapest.

We have Fedor's trail to Budapest. Just don't know where he went after leaving the airport.

Navalny's secretary ain't been of any use on this problem. She just knows that Fedor is ready to push all the buttons as soon as his counterpart-in-crime is ready to go.

Explained that to Darnell as well.

Now, I have one more complication here.

In addition to seeing my brother be successful, and preventing Putin from probably putting a bullet in Navalny's head, I've got skin in the game.

I've been working for Oleg Deripaska for the last two years.

Surprise!

It's actually a good deal. He doesn't ask what I do for a living and I don't request anything but pay from him. The deal works this way—I keep his corporate machines free of "outside visitors" and leave a very subtle reminder for one of his IT geeks about where to find would-be intruders.

Outside job that pays for Momma and Dad's vacations. Also covered the mortgage on their house. Then there's the medical costs I ran up after the motorcycle accident. That insurance us government people supposedly live the grand life on, it ain't that good. Baby, I got bills, and a girl's got to live. That Tesla wasn't cheap.

Deripaska's "recruiter" found me when I was busy hacking into a Russia-based dark website. Fingered me cold. You can back out and cover tracks in the digital world. If you're good. I'm damn good. And he still hunted me down. To the house. When Momma was sleeping upstairs. Bastard came to the front door. Knew I was awake, at 0235 in the morning. Only knocked once; Wiper heard him and barked.

Well, I answered. What the hell can you do? I knew who—at least digitally who—it was. No one else would expect me or any other sane person to be awake at that time of the night. Or would that be day? Shit it doesn't matter. He was standing there, with my 9mm pointed at his head.

"You want work?" That's all he asked. Left a card with a URL address. That's it.

I took the chance.

Deripaska pays well. Never demanding. The most frequent concern I hear from his man here in Washington—yes, that bastard who showed up at my front door lives somewhere up here on Capitol Hill—is what are the other oligarchs doing? Best I can tell there is bad, bad blood among the inner circle. Sharks waiting for the whale to die so they can divide the spoils.

Darnell doesn't know any of this shit.

I'm sure as hell not gonna tell him.

chapter

18

timed out

budapest, hungary, 5 october 2025

It's 0317 on a Sunday morning in Budapest. Looking out the hotel room one would conclude the city has gone to bed. There are few cars roaming the streets, taxis have disappeared, and there is no wailing of police or ambulance sirens. All observations Bakshi could not have made less than three hours ago. At 0030 on a Budapest Sunday morning it appeared all hell was breaking loose below her hotel room window. She'd forgotten the theatrics people engage in upon leaving a bar after a night of drinking and dancing. Montgomery didn't have much of a night scene. The Air Force discouraged such activities for its officers, and there were no major colleges or universities.

Budapest, at least from her vantage point, apparently knew how to party. Must be an Eastern European thing. She didn't know, never spent any time studying or reading about this part of the world. Nor had she been much of a party animal in the first place. Too busy studying. Oh, she'd go out for beers with the business partners on a rare occasion and had even been dancing in a Montgomery bar once or twice with men who were obviously focused on getting into her pants. Even took one home, once. Wasn't bad, wasn't great.

At the moment she wasn't thinking about dancing or drinking. She was ready to execute the next step in their plan. Fedor's promised "present" for the Bitcoin miners was "just about there."

He was definitely not her type. The incessant cigarette smoke left her reeking like an ashtray and his constant swearing—in English and Russian—was not endearing. At least he'd made no romantic overtures. She'd be more than a little tempted to knee him in the groin should such an eventuality develop. No reason to worry, Fedor was as disinterested in her as she was in him.

If asked, Fedor would admit a passion for busty Russian women with light, light skin. Preferably blond. At least that's what he surfed for on porn sites. She was none of those things. Probably weighed fifty kilos, had no tits, and was dark brown. To say nothing of the very black hair.

All to her advantage in this case. Made him focus on coding.

That promise some forty-two hours ago about being finished in four to five hours—a "coder's lie." An insider's way of explaining that what was to be delivered within a certain timeframe might take somewhere between three, four, or five times as long to complete. There was a sort of Murphy's Law associated with coding—the closer you got, the further away an objective became.

Fedor caught the target at 0348 on 5 October. With Bakshi watching over his shoulder, the email launched to over sixty thousand known Bitcoin miners scattered across the globe. All sent from Bitfinex.com.

Bitfinex advertised itself as "the world's largest and most advanced cryptocurrency trading platform." Launched in 2013, the firm claimed to have never been hacked, and was famous for holding 99.5 percent of client assets in "cold storage." That is to say, they sucked in cybercurrency, put the data on removable hard drives, and then disconnected the boxes from the web. Physically. They pulled the plug until a client requested access to his or her money.

Blockchain users trusted Bitfinex explicitly.

That was step one of Fedor's plan.

He'd put Bakshi to work on crafting the email. Step two. To the effect of:

> Greetings from Bitfinex,
> Our research shows you are a sophisticated participant in the cybercurrency community. As such, we suspect you expend a good deal of time and energy searching for the latest opportunity to acquire further holdings. In our silent partnership with the Gates Foundation, we have developed a more resource efficient means of "mining." This campaign is intended to protect our global environment and expand your opportunity to improve personal finances. The attached file provides all the information you will require. In exchange for this data, we humbly request you consider our services in the near future.
> Sincerely,
> Bitfinex

She had to admit, step three, the attached PDF file, was a work of coding art. If you clicked on the file—*perhaps* 5 percent of the email recipients would do so—nothing untoward happened. Instead, the page revealed a coding sequence which might actually work once executed. The file reeked of professional competence.

It also contained a bit of malware that none of the current antivirus or "security" programs would detect. Once the user opened the PDF, Fedor's worm crawled into their machine and went in search of the blockchain and Bitcoin access codes. After the required data was located, the program transmitted that information back to Fedor and Bakshi, then erased itself. That was step four.

Masterful. The targets would never know they'd been struck, nor would they be victims. That fate awaited the oligarchs. And just the three Bakshi had selected.

She watched as Fedor pulled the second USB drive from a dirty corner of a satchel and stuck it in his machine. In less than five minutes he'd drafted an email to each of the target recipients. The format was done in a manner suggesting each was a unique delivery, not a mass mailing. This would fool few of the recipients. If they were indeed mining Bitcoin, they were smart enough to understand how email can be tailored to disguise spam.

But it was from Bitfinex. The email "from" line was not an obscure "edu" extension or indicative of a Nigerian hoax.

"How many hits do you need?" He finally said something, after silently working away for hours.

"Thirty-five. All in China. Then I execute the transactions through their machines. And subsequently shut off the power. Should give us the 51 percent required for this maneuver."

Temporarily deprived of all those transaction histories, the remaining miners would keep operating. Once the power came back on, the new transaction history should flood the system. Giving Navalny exactly what he'd requested.

Fedor took another vodka swig. "I'm going to sleep." A gruff announcement. Seemingly a statement intended to make her leave his room. "Doctor"—he was slurring now, too tired and more than a little drunk—"I set an alarm on your machine. When you hit thirty-five suckers it will go off. Unless you shut down the computer, it can't be missed."

Conveniently, he then passed out atop a litter of room service dishes and his own dirty clothes. Was snoring before she made it to the room's door.

To hack is to live. And to live, is, of course, to hack.

Bakshi drew the curtains in her room. The view was spectacular, but she had no interest in being awakened at daybreak. She'd hung a "Do Not Disturb" sign on the outside door handle and called the front desk to ensure there would be no knock for maid service. Brushed her teeth, stripped off the cigarette-smoked clothing. Stood in the shower for a few minutes and found her pajamas. Like a civilized person she then slid beneath the sheets and fell quite dead asleep.

The damn computer went off with Russian martial music at 1112 Budapest time, scared her awake with a start that resulted in blankets being tossed on the floor. Bakshi dashed to the machine, hunting for a volume button. Took a moment to gather her senses and realize what this meant. Fedor's phishing had worked, all too well. She looked up the time transition. It was 1812 in Beijing. Evening on a Sunday. Hopefully traffic would be light.

She now had log-in access for more than four hundred blockchain users. Took a few minutes to discover Fedor had already set up her machine to automatically start building an access file with each of his "suckers." That made step five in the plan relatively simple.

She fired off the transaction request at 1148 Budapest time.

Five minutes later she shut out the lights for 210 million Chinese, called room service, requested an oolong tea and light sandwich.

washington, dc, 5 october 2025

Who the hell calls you at 0630 on a Sunday? Momma knows the gym doesn't open until 0700 and I don't bother to slide out of bed until 0715. The gym can wait until 0900. By then I've had a chance to read the *Washington Post* front page and consider the mountain that the *New York Times* disgorges on every sabbath. Go get out your dictionary, sabbath is the Lord's decreed day of rest. At least if you're Christian; that would be Sunday. Friday if you're Muslim, Saturday if you're Jewish. You can use that bit of trivia at the next cocktail party.

Now, I am none of the above, but Sunday is slow at my house. I always expect a call about 0800. Momma asking if I am coming to church. I've said no for the last ten years. She still tries every Sunday. Give the woman credit, probably where I learned to be so stubborn.

It wasn't 0800, it was 0630. What the fuck?

Phone keeps ringing. Going to have to answer.

Reach over to the nightstand. Have to push Wiper out of the way; damn dog thinks he's some sort of five-pound Yorkie and took to sleeping on my bed. Snores, farts, and takes all the covers. Worse than a few of the men I've let in over the years. My fault, I never pushed him off after night one, kind of like the company. Plus, if Wiper lurches into alert mode in the middle of the night, well, that means I'm also wide awake.

Grab the phone. Look for caller ID. There was none. Shit. I know who this is.

Work.

They don't even wait for hello, just launch right in as soon as the connection goes live.

"Darnell thinks he has the Big Dog."

I know how this game goes. "Penned or leashed?"

"Penned." Click.

That meant Darnell found Fedor's hotel. "Leashed" would be a whole different matter.

Let me fill you in here. Darnell was dispatched with a list of accommodations, instructed to locate the one where Fedor is likely staying and then give the Russian a free ride to transportation that would leave him in a much warmer climate. Specifically, Gitmo Camp Seven. That would be the secret detention facility with Guantanamo Bay facilities. You know, as in our prisons set up on Cuba to keep terrorists and a few other unfriendly actors out of the U.S. legal system.

To pull this off, Darnell flew into Budapest, rented a very nice Mercedes-Benz sedan (I know motorcycles, I could give a shit about cars, I just know Mercedes makes expensive ones—and Darnell never rents cheap shit, I've seen his expense accounts). Meanwhile, Ops set up a deal with the Air Force to have a KC-10, a large refueling aircraft, sitting on the runway at their base in Aviano, Italy. Darnell makes his pickup, hopefully identifies Fedor's accomplice, and then drops the Russian, and maybe a "guest," off with the flyboys. Just requires driving through Hungary, Austria, and a bit of Italy. This is Europe, not the United States. Go get out a map.

Oh, and he gets to do that with Fedor in the trunk, stuffed in a duffel bag and stoned on horse sedative.

Piece of cake, right?

One little problem. Have to get Fedor out of a hotel room without drawing a crowd. Or, worse yet, possible backup. As in security assigned to keep Fedor out of our hands. Oh, and do this as a very large black man in a very pasty-white Eastern European country.

I can bitch about my job. But Darnell isn't exactly riding easy street.

(I asked him later about how he blended into the population in Budapest. His response was "Bad European clothes and all the Middle Eastern refugees." Guess there might be some people of color in Hungary after all.)

Phone rang again. Same absence of caller ID.

This time they were polite. "You watching the news?"

"No, was trying to sleep."

"Might want to." They hung up again.

This time I did push Wiper off my bed. Pull the chair over and roll into the bathroom. Hey, you sleep all night and not get up to pee in the morning? Yeah, thought that was the answer. Brush my teeth, try to drag a pick through my hair and then tug on gym clothes.

Roll out to the front door, grab the newspapers—I got the delivery man trained, he leaves them up on the top stoop where I can get the crap without having to go down that lift machine. At this point I roll back to the kitchen and start my coffee routine. Turn on the TV. Feed Wiper and let him out in back. More fertilizer for the garden. Remind myself to get Darnell's kids over here to do some pooper-scooping.

Coffee dribbles out into a cup. I spin around and turn the volume up on CNN.

Bad karma.

Power out all over China.

That happens only one way. My world, the hacker community. Death count is already estimated at over a thousand. Chinese officials are blaming Washington. Telling reporters this is part of President Schumer's ongoing trade wars. Threatening to respond in kind. Oh, shit.

Another phone call. Same unlisted number.

"Darnell has a passenger."

"Just one?" My question.

"Just one." End of call.

Well, baby brother done good. Told you he had an interesting job.

budapest, hungary, 5 october 2025

Bakshi guessed it must have been about 1330 on Sunday when she heard a door shut in the hallway. It wasn't slammed, just quietly closed like any decent guest would do. Then it dawned on her, that might be Fedor going out. She had no idea when he was scheduled to depart. Their job here was done. Good riddance, as far as she was concerned.

She slipped on clean clothes, placed the old laundry in a hotel-provided bag, and called the front desk. "Please have them come make up my room and take the cleaning."

"Yes, ma'am."

With that she walked out. Probably no less than five to ten minutes after she'd heard the door close.

Darnell returned three minutes after she'd left. Missed her in the hallway or getting on the elevator. Didn't know that. He slid the keycard into her door and did a quick walkthrough. The dirty laundry confirmed Fedor's counterpart in crime was a woman, a small woman. That's all he could tell from the belongings. He scooped up the laptop and walked out. Took the elevator back down to the InterContinental's underground parking garage.

Fedor had been easier to handle than expected. The Russian was obviously sleep-deprived and still drunk. The injection of tizanidine—a muscle relaxant and sleep aid—knocked him out immediately. Would need a booster shot when Darnell stopped for gas in Austria. Meanwhile, he could sleep in the Mercedes's trunk.

Darnell tossed the second laptop on the passenger seat. Fedor's was already stowed beneath his jacket on the rear bench. Time to leave. The big man said a silent thanks for the Hungarian contractor who had not bothered to place security cameras in the underground garage. And then smiled at the thought of the look on the desk clerk's face upon discovering she could earn $500 American just by revealing where a certain Russian guest, who checked in on the 2 October, might be staying in the hotel.

She'd recognized Fedor's picture. Even mentioned his travel partner, one Adya Bakshi, was staying in an adjoining room. Fedor, the young lady volunteered, was in 612, the woman was in 610. He'd thanked her. Then walked off. Seemingly a businessman out to meet acquaintances for a late lunch.

Bakshi returned to the room about three hours later. She'd walked four blocks to the Anna Café for a pastry and fresh juice. Then toured a bit. Probably would never be back in Budapest, might as well take advantage of the moment.

Returned to find the room immaculate, clothes apparently taken to the cleaners. And then noticed the missing computer. Strange,

Fedor did not have a key to her room; he swore that up and down when Bakshi verbally worried he would let himself in when she was sleeping. The hotel maids knew better than to steal a machine of that value. Guaranteed near immediate prosecution. But someone had been here in her absence.

The tingling feeling was much worse than before. She contacted the Delta reservations desk and requested a return flight on 6 October. Claimed she felt very ill. She did, and that was before flicking on the TV to catch up with the news.

chapter 19

aces and eights ... play with your back to a wall

moscow, russia, 16 october 2025

Navalny knew. Shit, he'd been responsible for the phone calls. *He'd* made the phone calls. Hence, it was not terribly surprising that Fedor did not appear after the attorney used a disposable burner to send a single word message, "Available," to the hacker. Little doubt in his mind where Fedor was located. Guantanamo. The place where Americans made people go disappear. Washington's version of the "vanished."

This he did know: Fedor had been successful.

Rumors swirled during political gatherings of a turf war in the *okruzheniya.* Word was out that Oleg Deripaska was down to a paltry few million—used to be $8 billion—Yuri Kovalchuck, broke, somehow managed to squander $1.5 billion, and Igor Sechin was supposedly now borrowing from his counterparts running Rosneft. Those kinds of financial losses don't stay buried. Particularly when the apparent victims spent hours shouting into phones demanding answers about where the fuck their money went.

Secretaries have ears and like to whisper the latest news to their closest confidants. Who, of course, go on to share the chitchat with their confidants. Doesn't take long for stories of a bedroom fiasco to make it through a neighborhood. Imagine the speed with which this kind of development dashes about a city like Moscow. A city where being on the inside meant make or break for a career, family, and fortune.

There were also whispers that Washington was responsible. Nasty comments to the effect President Schumer—that damn Jew—was trying to exercise the Dulles Doctrine. Navalny had been around long enough to know what that meant. It was folklore from back in the days of Brezhnev. Supposedly, in the late 1950s, Allen Dulles, then head of the CIA, crafted a plan to destroy the Soviet Union by corrupting its social moral values and deriding Russia's cultural heritage. Instead of financially bankrupting the "evil empire," Ronald Reagan's plan, Dulles was said to be preparing the Russians for a descent into societal hubris no dictator could avert.

Think of the disaster Mao created with his Cultural Revolution. That was the Dulles Doctrine. Or so many common citizens of Moscow believed.

He could see the logic in reaching this assumption. If Putin's *okruzheniya* could be pulled apart, robbed, and pitted against one another—well, what would happen to the rest of Russian society? Sadly, reminded him of an old joke: "In America, you go to mob. In Russia, mob comes to you." It just took someone to start the mob. Just as Putin had tried to do with the American elections in 2016, 2018, and again in 2020.

Never seemed to work as planned. Well, once. Donald Trump did occupy the White House. At least four days a week for a few years. The rest of his time seemed to be spent at golf courses. That was no win for the Kremlin. And was certainly not mentioned in front of Putin. Just became the source for another Russian joke: "In Russia, government screw you. In America, president screw government!"

Now, in Russia, the oligarchs were screwing one another.

His secretary would return from her second's meeting with news of gun battles among the billionaires' security goons and even outright attempts to push Putin into using legal measures to seize one man's assets from another.

Exactly, Navalny mused, what Vladimir Vladimirovich Putin desired. He wanted a blood-letting and disintegration of the ranks. Then Putin could walk away with little fear of a putsch.

If he lived that long. His secretary also spoke of assassination plots passed along by her SVR paramour. Seems more than one of the *okruzheniya* suspected Vladimir was guilty of causing these sudden financial woes. And seemed to have little interest in keeping the inner circle from devouring its own.

How close they were to the truth. And how far they were from realizing the consequences. Navalny would purge the lot in his first month sitting in that chair Putin currently occupied. Use the same technique that stripped Deripaska. He bet he could barter Fedor out of Guantanamo. Just needed to ensure SVR grabbed the right American asset.

Here's where his ploy in working with the CIA had paid off. The CIA station chief in Moscow treated Navalny like royalty. A stupid American bid to develop leverage over a man they reasoned could not be a president, but obviously knew how to get under a Russian leader's skin. Went so far as to offer Navalny a glimpse into the Embassy's prized jewels—the men and women who collected intelligence on the Russian government.

Yes, Navalny knew exactly who could be traded for Fedor. If the poor bastard lived that long.

He said nothing to his secretary. Nodded approval at her work with Putin's second and instructed preparation of a batch of emails to be sent out to his fellow patriots combating the oligarch corruption and thievery. Best not to tip his hand too soon. And he would never let her know of his connections with Washington.

She, of course, maintained the same discretion in dealing with him. Her CIA handler had already promised a house in South Carolina when it came time to flee Mother Russia.

montgomery, alabama, 17 october 2025

Bakshi had finally gone to a doctor for her insomnia. Her eyes had dark rings under them, clothes barely fit—she required a belt to keep jeans from sliding off her waist. Hired a local locksmith to come and install a second deadbolt—didn't tell the apartment management. She didn't want anyone else to have keys to her residence.

For good reason. Bakshi was now a mass murderer.

Pulling the power on 210 million Chinese had resulted in more than 3,200 deaths. Or so the officials in Beijing claimed. There was an international campaign underway to discover and capture the culprit. No national government could allow for such behavior. In fact, President Schumer had been one of the first to go on television to declare a war on such cyber "perversions."

Her fear was well founded. Snowden had revealed the extent to which NSA could reach into a hacker's livelihood. LoudAuto—a program that activated a laptop's microphone without alerting the machine's owner—monitored all accessible conversations. HowlerMonkey pulled out files and transmitted them to a nearby location via radio signals—even if the computer wasn't attached to the internet. MonkeyCalendar traced a cell phone's location and fed the data back to an intended recipient via text messages. NightStand was a mobile system that could implant malware on a target machine from miles away. And then there was RageMaster, a means of allowing remote monitoring of anything she displayed.

Strangely, it was this paranoia of being watched, listened to, and hacked that caused the sleeplessness. The deaths ceased to nag after a few days. These were fatalities far from her location. The bereaved families and outraged newspaper headlines did not touch front doorsteps in Montgomery. It was similar to hearing about a typhoon killing thousands in the Philippines. Sad, but nothing you could do about it. Life went on.

No, the sleeplessness was of her own doing. With Fedor gone, Bakshi had two diversions absorbing her attention. The first was a digital storage device locked in a safe bolted to her bedroom closet floor. By her calculations it was the code for over $3.2 billion she'd diverted from Deripaska's Bitcoin wallet. Like Bitfinex, she believed in "cold storage." There was no requirement to rush forward with expenditures or further redistribution of the wealth. It would only draw attention.

She'd pushed the remaining funds—a total of somewhere in the vicinity of $6 billion—into various charities and minor Russian political movements. Nothing went to Navalny's Anti-Corruption Foundation; Bakshi worried that would have drawn undue attention. Fedor had mentioned Navalny was always short on money. Bakshi had seen enough Indian and American politicians ruined by a sudden flood of cash to understand it was best to leave the Russian attorney poor—at least for the moment.

The second cause of her sleep deprivation was that Bakshi now wondered who was running Endless Horizons.

This was a surprising development. Uncertain that Fedor would honor her request to be spared future demands for computing services and leave her hard-earned reputation intact, she'd spent hours disassembling his firewall in a manner that even the "master" failed to notice. Dr. Bakshi had broken through less than a week before their meeting in Budapest, and was astounded. Fedor was making $65 million a year serving as little more than a middleman between the clients and producers.

All the business was done through his servers and only he knew who the clients were and who the producers might be. Transactions all accomplished in cybercurrencies. Her job was to hold the transactions until the goods were delivered and then push the payment into blockchain—retaining a 10 percent cut for each deal. There were, needless to say, a lot of transactions. Thousands on a given day. Fortunately, Fedor had developed the code necessary to automate the process. Otherwise, she would need a room full of support staff.

Automated, but not fully. There were some transactions (those totaling over $15,000, and sensitive requests—certain unpleasant "services") that required her personal approval. They would hang in an administrative que, then trigger a text on her phone. "You've got mail." The old Yahoo greeting. Fedor likely thought it was funny. She found the texts annoying, but necessary. Even with the criteria Fedor had imposed, there were often ten to fifteen such requests every day.

Which necessitated a trip to a public wi-fi provider. Like the "Dread Pirate Roberts," the founder of Silk Road who was now serving a life sentence without possibility of parole, she chose public libraries. There were fourteen in Montgomery, if you counted four of the nearby county branches. Which meant she could move from one location to another during the week without drawing attention to the amount of time spent on the internet rather than perusing bound slips of paper.

Hardly unique. There were a fair number of people who showed up with their laptops and then spent hours online. The library sought to keep unseemly surfing to a minimum with restrictions on the websites that could (or should) be accessed in a public place. That worked, sort of. Bakshi had seen more than one less-than-covert act of masturbation at the back tables of some smaller branches that had few staff to monitor the riffraff.

The tingle in her head was now so loud she never dared turn on a laptop in her apartment. Was convinced NSA or SVR were simply waiting to verify her activities. For all she knew, it could also be the CIA or China's Ministry of State Security. She'd warned her business partners of these fears without explaining why. Nor did she mention Endless Horizons. Simply declared a requirement for a couple more weeks off and then said her phone number had changed and she would only speak with them face-to-face. Once a week at a rotating chain of restaurants.

"Dude, you in trouble with the feds?" A singular question from the older of her two business partners.

"Just being cautious." That's all she could say.

What she failed to mention was the fact that Endless Horizons now seemed to operate without her interface. And funds were starting to disappear into the ether. There was obviously another player in this game.

washington, dc, 17 october 2025

Indian bitch was being careful, I'll give her that. Slunk back into this country with no electronics and then went home to Montgomery. Montgomery, Alabama. Why the fuck would a nice Indian girl move to Alabama? You know how those crackers treat people of color? Well, maybe it's changed, ain't been down there in a good while. Never see a reason. Sure, I get to fly through Atlanta regularly, but Alabama, no thanks.

Didn't matter where she snuck off to, we were on her like stink on shit. Give her credit. Seemed to stay off the web. At least where NSA set up collections. I don't think she even turned on her cell phone in that apartment. Left the place all the time. I know that because we tasked the FBI with following her about.

Public libraries and Starbucks. Should have guessed. Looking for wi-fi in all the free spaces. Locales where there's enough clutter coming through a router to potentially bury her traffic. "Potentially." Baby, we got a lot of money running through NSA and CYBERCOM. Only had to ask the boss once before attorneys from CIA, FBI, and NSA were requesting wiretaps from the Foreign Intelligence Surveillance Court (FISC).

The kids from NSA set up intercepts in every one of Montgomery's public libraries. Shit, that's how they got the Dread Pirate Roberts of Silk Road fame. Don't these people read the newspaper or learn their own cyber history? Really? I was becoming less impressed by the good Dr. Bakshi by the hour.

Oh, justified all this through the court on a suspicion she was responsible for the SCADA attack in China and could be preparing the same here in the United States of America. That got the judge's attention.

Did I mention these requests for a wiretap in front of the FISC take place in a sealed courtroom? Yeah, can say things the press would love to hear, but will never be able to access. Try putting in a freedom of information request for actions taken under the Foreign Intelligence Surveillance Act. Might as well go pee in the wind or pull on Superman's cape. Ain't happening.

I mention Fedor yet? Nope. Don't worry, I haven't forgotten about Fedor.

Darnell delivered him to Aviano in less than eighteen hours. Man must have been driving 110 miles an hour. Well, it is Europe, seems they don't worry about fools who are set on killing themselves on a highway.

The USAF was kind enough to drop Fedor at Gitmo. Darnell? Shit, he flew home first class. Brought his kids some interesting T-shirts and surprised his wife with a selection of fine Italian cheeses and prosciutto. I give my brother credit. He knows how to keep that woman happy, despite his "business excursions."

Seems Fedor's not so delighted with his spot at Gitmo. No silk sheets. And he sure as hell did *not* like waterboarding. Couldn't stop talking after the second session. So, yes, we know about the Bitcoin escapade, we know about the ties to Navalny, and we know Navalny has it in for Putin's inner circle. Hell, baby, we even know about Endless Horizons. Meanwhile, have the digital forensic types at NSA busy using those two laptops Darnell brought back to unravel Fedor's coding. See, that Russian boy was even nice enough to divulge all his passwords.

Told you waterboarding works.

What we don't know is where all that money went. Fedor made some guesses. Haven't been able to confirm them. We don't know who Dr. Bakshi targeted among the Russian oligarchs, and we don't know who's currently running Endless Horizons, but it sure as hell has not been shut down.

Explained some of that to the FISC judge, made the process go even smoother than expected. Had wiretap permissions in less than four hours. Now it's just a matter of catching Dr. Bakshi in a criminal act. Just a matter of time, she'll slip. They all do, except me.

Momma always lectures me, "pride before the fall." Then she reminds me of the motorcycle accident and this damn chair. I just smile; no use in arguing with Momma. Plus, she still drops by to leave leftovers in my fridge. Who has time to cook these days? Only retired people.

Here's my problem. Deripaska wants his money back.

Made that perfectly clear when his SVR buddy who lives somewhere in my neighborhood—think I told you about him—came by to visit. At 0245. Came clean through my alarm system, hit Wiper with a tranquilizer dart, and was sitting in my living room before I could get on the chair, pull a weapon, and roll around the hallway corner.

Pretty simple instructions: "Your services are required."

Don't need to say more. No good in my being pissed with him. He's just a messenger boy. But if he ever pulls that shit on Wiper again there's going to be hell to pay. I'll shoot his white ass and then tell the police I had a B and E problem. A woman's entitled to defend her castle. Even in DC these days.

Time to go to work. Can't be sitting here talking story with you people. Only going to get another hour of sleep before it's gym time and then a run at Dr. Bakshi's coding skills. Want to see who's better? Pride before the fall, baby. Pride before the fall.

chapter

20

digital accounting

montgomery, alabama, 19 october 2025

Bakshi's doctor prescribed temazepam—also known as Restoril—in a thirty-milligram dosage. Warned her it was also a muscle relaxant; he used it as a sedative before surgeries. She was going to be "out," as he put it, for eight to ten hours every time one slid down her throat.

"Don't combine it with booze, unless you want to lose a day. Or a week, or your life."

No worries there, she had zero intention of committing suicide. Just needed the sleep to think clearly. It was time to plan a rapid departure from Montgomery. The tingling became worse by the day. And now she was convinced somebody, or somebodies, were watching her every move. She never spotted a car or van that caused suspicion, but in the back of her mind there was a silent alarm that never turned off. Became so bad Bakshi checked into the Renaissance Montgomery Hotel on Friday night. Stayed on Saturday as well. Most expensive place in town. Had great wi-fi, uniformed guards were constantly present, and she was able to hack into the camera security system in about fifteen minutes.

Took a taxi from her apartment, left the car behind to throw off a possible trail.

Reminded herself about fifteen times she could afford this. No, actually, Bakshi could afford to *live* in the Renaissance Hotel if she so desired. Used to be a fashionable thing to do. Back in the late nineteenth and early twentieth centuries. This was the twenty-first century; people didn't live in hotels any more. Would just draw attention to herself.

Took a temazepam at 0230 on Saturday morning. Woke at 1015. Best sleep she'd had in a week, tingling gone. Ordered tea and a bowl of grits with fresh fruit on the side for breakfast. Then logged back into the laptop. Time to do business.

Darnell was sitting in the back of a delivery van with five of his best NSA "friends." Truck was wrapped in advertisements for Colonial Bread. Used to be a staple here—good old-fashioned white bread, best served with peanut butter and jelly. Now it was relegated to the back shelves. Seemed everyone wants whole wheat or some fancy French roll. Didn't matter, the Colonial trucks still ran all over town. They blended in.

Didn't hurt they'd run the vehicle down a few gravel roads to acquire the right amount of dirt on its exterior. No delivery van is pristine. Unless it's being used for surveillance.

That little excursion made the NSA boys wince. Afraid of banging up delicate equipment. No problem. Darnell slowed down for the worst potholes. In any case, the gear was all secured to racks. As soon as they finished here the truck would be driven into the back end of a C-17 parked at Maxwell Air Force Base and flown to Baltimore International. From there it would be taken to Fort Meade to be cleaned and prepped for the next job. NSA had one of the "wrap" guys on their payroll, even bought all his equipment. Just printed out new advertisements to be pasted on the truck and flew it to another location.

At this stage they were simply waiting for Bakshi to go online. The FBI had agents standing by to make the arrest.

Monitored her emails and transactions for sixteen hours straight.

Then watched it all shut down.

"Collection time." Darnell's only comment for the entire day.

He walked into the hotel, signaled the FBI field agents, obtained a key card from the front desk, and rode the elevator to floor seven. Room 715. Swiped once and walked in. Bakshi was comatose. Bottle of sleeping pills on the night stand, remnants of a dinner salad and glass of wine on the room's desk. Along with her computer.

She was beyond groggy when they clamped on the handcuffs. Darnell grabbed the laptop. Searched for any other paperwork and then walked out behind the two FBI types half-dragging, half-walking Bakshi to the elevator and then out to the delivery truck.

"One more stop." They knew where.

He kicked in the door. The FBI was going to be here a while, he was not. That plane was taking off with the van, him, the NSA crew, and Bakshi. Law enforcement guys could handle cleanup in Montgomery.

Darnell thoroughly ransacked Dr. Bakshi's apartment. Not a hard job. Was largely bare. What she did own fell into the category of well-organized.

Found the safe in her bedroom closet. Darnell wasn't about to open it. His son had a cross-country race on Sunday at noon, up in Maryland. He planned to be there.

Back at the delivery truck: "Got a tire iron?" Of course, the computer geeks had no idea. He searched through the van. There it was.

Back up to the apartment. Hooked one end of the tire iron under the safe and gave it a healthy yank. Plywood floor parted company with the lag bolts. Apartment manager was going to make some handyman a happy person. Had to be $400 of work between the door and the floor. More, after the feds got done pulling things apart. Shit, might be $1,500 worth of work in here by then.

Darnell hoisted the mini-safe on his shoulder and walked

out—damn things only weigh about 150 pounds. Passed one of the FBI agents smoking a cigarette at the bottom of the steps.

"Rest is yours." Put the safe on the floor at the rear entrance of the van. Closed the doors. Bakshi was handcuffed to a rack, looked like she was asleep again.

"Roll." His final comment.

The C-17 left at 0400, precisely.

He'd make his son's cross-country race.

Barely.

washington, dc, 22 october 2025

Well, look what little brother brought me. No, you dummy, not Dr. Bakshi, let the feds deal with her. Now I had another laptop and standalone backup drive. Said right on the side it could store up to a terabyte. Maybe more, the manufacturers tended to underestimate. That was particularly true if you knew how to compress data and optimize a hard drive.

The real trick is getting into these toys.

That was an operation I wanted to do at home. In the privacy of my own office. Signed for the gear—what, you thought they'd let me just roll out with material likely to be used in a criminal investigation? Don't be silly. The CIA has rules about this kind of thing. Plus, the FBI was all over ensuring they got the boxes back. The agents down south were more than a little pissed when Darnell just took off with Bakshi and the evidence. Too bad. Bunch of old-fashioned, buttoned-up, white men stuck in Alabama. They'll get over it. And they'll get this shit back when I'm done. Hell, we gave them Dr. Bakshi; that ought to be worth something. Been up to me, Darnell would have parked her in a cell next to Fedor down in Gitmo. Bet that would have made for some interesting taped conversations.

Instead, she's in some maximum-security facility the FBI refuses to discuss down in Quantico. That's south of DC, go look it up. Damn, I got to do everything for you?

Dr. Bakshi's not the only one living an interesting life these days. The NSA folks have been providing no end of fascinating reading from Moscow. Seems the oligarchs are engaged in a real Hatfields-and-McCoys feud. Reports of shootings, enraged phone calls, endless accusations, and even a bit of arson. The NGA guys came in with some great overhead shots of torched dachas. No dead rich men, yet. But, hell, they're Russian. Sooner or later one of them, maybe more, are gonna die.

My aging Russian analyst claims Putin is now sitting in a "lonely room." Of his own making. The old man, when he's not wheezing, thinks Putin initiated this internecine warfare to clean house. Perhaps to open the door for a new crop of loyalists he can manipulate even more fully than the last group.

That bit of analysis caused quite an argument in the Dog Pound. Seems the kids from NSA, NGA, and INR don't agree. They think Putin is planning to take the money and run. The man does look worn out. Not having fun anymore. He's just clearing the ground, so Dmitry Medvedev can come back for another term as president. You remember Medvedev, was the Russian president from May 2008 to May 2012? All so Putin wouldn't violate the country's constitution by serving more than two consecutive terms in the front office.

Medvedev is a real lapdog. That's what George Will, the whacky conservative columnist, called George Bush the First. Like Bush, Medvedev probably gets out of the shower to pee. And, always does what Putin instructs. Same thing Bush did for Ronald Reagan.

Yeah, yeah, dragging your ass through ancient history. Baby, you got to know this stuff.

Oh, we ain't heard shit from Navalny since all this went down. His secretary still talks with the CIA connections in Moscow. Claims the man didn't make a dime out of this whole racket. He's still apparently engaged in rooting out corruption and planning a run in the March 2026 Russian presidential election.

Sometimes I really wonder why we pay these sources. I could have told you that.

All right, time to roll. Have the computer and backup drive in a bag, placed it on my lap. The security guys tend to leave us "handicapped" alone.

Let's see what presents Dr. Bakshi delivered.

moscow, russia, 28 october 2025

Navalny left his office for lunch. Told his secretary he was going to meet his wife, it was their wedding anniversary. Twenty-fifth anniversary of "tying the knot," as Americans put it. He'd purchased a silver bracelet designed by David Yurman. Simple, yet elegant. Exactly her taste. Made reservations at White Rabbit. Her favorite place. Spectacular view of Moscow, food was a combination of traditional Russian and Italian. Chef always had a new dish on as a special. Made reservations weeks before—otherwise it was impossible to get a table.

He opted for a cab. It would have been a long walk in the rain. Not impossible, but why be wet and cold? Plus, it gave him time to make a phone call, or two, or three. Conversations the driver could overhear. But was out of his secretary's earshot. She'd become increasingly nosy. This one did not need to go into whatever set of notes she was keeping. Yes, he'd noticed the pages with lines of cryptic script. Something was afoot. Another problem to address. After his lunch, and perhaps a little romance—there was a nearby hotel. That brought a smile to his face.

Yet another burner. Such a waste of money. But if you don't want the CIA, FSB, NSA, and SVR listening to your calls, well, throw away the cash.

First call was to Channel One, the most popular television station in Russia. Broadcast out of a studio located near the Ostankino Tower, tallest structure in Europe—a remnant of the Soviet Union. He requested a young man who answered the call patch him through to the news desk. A ploy that only worked after he explained this was *the* Alexei Navalny.

The operator patched him through.

An exchange of greetings, obviously an editor seeking stories for the next news broadcast. That would be at 2200. Yes, there was an earlier version, with a very small audience. Everyone tuned into social media for breaking stories these days.

"I'm going to make an announcement in Red Square, 1700, today, in front of Spasskaya Tower. You will want to have a camera crew there." Navalny's abrupt pronouncement.

"Can I ask what this is about?" A new editor trying to justify sending out a team to take footage of a man everyone *knew* was despised inside the Kremlin.

"No. I'm just saying, you will want coverage. I am giving you, how do they say, an 'exclusive.' And I will not be alone."

Navalny hung up, then made the same call to NTV, REN-TV, Russia Today, and STS. Everyone was offered an "exclusive" and the promise he would not be alone. Then he started calling newspapers. Started with *Izvestia,* on to the *Moscow Times,* and finished with the *New York Times.* Same story line he'd spieled to Channel One.

The cab driver was obviously soaking all this in. "You are really Alexei Navalny?" Asked in an incredulous manner.

"Da."

"Then why aren't your people making these calls? I would think you are too busy for such work."

"Some things are best left to the boss." By now they'd been parked curbside in front of the restaurant for fifteen minutes. Navalny wanted to complete his phone calls in private... or at least, just in front of the cab driver. He paid the man, provided a generous tip, and then requested nothing further be said of his conversations. Was greeted with a nod of agreement.

With that he walked up to the lobby door, took the elevator up to the sixteenth floor and requested to be placed at the table with his wife. A striking, petite blond who'd given birth to his two children and put up with the political travails and multiple arrests for a quarter of a century. Only a few men get so lucky. She seemed to still love him. He was doing better than Putin on that front.

Delightful lunch. The "dessert" served a short block away in a nondescript hotel was even better.

Clock read 1535 when they'd showered and dressed.

"I have one more event today." His means of trying to reassure her.

"Another arrest?" A logical question. Navalny knew the back of police cars almost as well as the seats in Moscow's taxi fleet.

"Not this time." It came out of him so calmly.

She glanced up. Stared into his eyes. Then nodded. "I'll be at home. The children want to come for dinner to celebrate our anniversary. They're doing the cooking. Said about eight o'clock, don't be late." A modest chastising; he was notorious for never being on time.

"No promises." Spoken with a smile.

"I know." And with that she left.

Navalny finished adjusting his tie, polished his shoes one last time, and walked out about ten minutes behind her. Asked a new cab driver to take him to the office. Where he spent perhaps five minutes tapping away at the keyboard. Reading email and then offering replies. Or, so his secretary thought.

At 1610 Navalny slipped out the door, never muttered a word. His secretary presumed he would not be back. Not unusual. Long ago Navalny had made sure lockup was her responsibility. Done with the daily administrative duties, she clicked on a television, turned to the news channel, and sat back to watch the daily update—a matter of killing time before closing up at 1730, the official end of the organization's business day.

Wasn't really paying attention to the talking heads until there was excitement about breaking news. Came at 1655. Something about Alexei Navalny making a big announcement in the next five minutes. The camera cut away to show a crowd of journalists and a mounting mob of average citizens starting to gather in front of Spasskaya Tower in Red Square.

Not a subtle place for a political statement. Spasskaya Tower had been the traditional entrance to the Kremlin. The tsars had demanded men remove their caps and dismount when passing through the gate. Stalin found the structure such a landmark he'd demanded the two eagles atop the tower be removed and replaced with a large red star. The gate and star were still there. As was the tower's emotional significance for an average Russian—it was *the* portal to power.

Promptly at 1700 Navalny walked in front of the microphones, pulling out a single note card.

He read: "Today, 108 years after 'Red October,' I come to proclaim a new revolution in Russia. Today, 28 October, I announce my candidacy for the Russian presidency. I do so with an understanding it is a long road and I must win the people's trust."

With that he stopped and turned to face the tower and its gates. They opened, as if on cue. It was—and a vehicle began to pass through. Not unheard of, the gate still served as an access point.

But what came out was immediately recognized as Putin's Project Cortege armored limousine. A turbocharged black sedan rumored to have over 600 horsepower.

The car rapidly accelerated, took an immediate left turn ten feet behind Navalny, and came to an abrupt halt.

No one said anything. The cameras kept running.

Navalny's secretary spoke aloud to the TV.

"What the *pizda rulyu!*" (What the fuck, we're screwed now.)

The boss was more than adept at getting arrested, but this was absurd. The government was going to take him away in Putin's limo? Well, it is Russia.

What happened next made news around the planet. Putin climbed out of the back seat. Walked up to Navalny and shook his hand. The Russian leader no longer had a spring in his step. Without the makeup usually applied for a television appearance his face was obviously lined and gray. A man who'd done his service. It was someone else's turn.

The Russian president stepped in front of Navalny, took his place before the cameras. "What you see next to me is the man I believe should be the next president of Russia. I will not be running in March. Nor will Mr. Medvedev."

With that he turned around, walked back to the car, climbed in the rear seat, and slammed shut the door. Putin's limousine reentered the tower gate and then the portal was promptly sealed.

"Are there questions?" Navalny asked, trying to suppress his smile.

washington, dc, 28 october 2025

"What the fuck?!"

First words out of the Dog Pound watch team member watching Navalny's performance. "Did Putin just quit?"

"No, young man." The old Russian analyst doing his shift, waiting for a morning meeting with the Veterinarian. "He just passed the throne to his chosen successor. Now we discover what really drives Alexei Navalny. You should pray it is not god, mother Russia, or wealth."

epilogue

chain of custody

washington, dc, 18 december 2025

Week before Christmas, have no damn shopping done. That's not true, just don't know what I'll get Darnell's kids. Already have a present for him and his wife. Reserved and paid for a long weekend at the Homestead in Hot Springs, Virginia. Set them up for early May 2026. Even found a babysitter to take care of the kids while they escape. Me. Darnell loves golf, his wife will never leave the spa. I took care of greens fees and the spa costs as well.

Think I'll get his kids a new 3-D TV with Microsoft's latest version of the Xbox. That, and another dog leash. After sitting on their ass all day playing games on a screen they're going to need that Wiper walk time. Bet I won points with their parents on that last purchase. The TV and Xbox, hell, that's Darnell's problem.

Took care of Momma and Dad already. Gave them an early Christmas and purchased a second Tesla SUV. Gave them mine. After it was completely gone over and detailed. Made Momma cry. Told her it was all right, they gave me a bonus at work. Well, they did. For "outstanding service." A check totaling $2,500. Around here that might buy a decent meal. What the hell is wrong with our government? Spend $800 billion on defense, give me an award for $2,500.

Can't bitch too much. Deripaska was all too happy to see $2.5 billion flow back into his new Bitcoin wallet. Gave me a gratuity award of $150,000. I never did have the heart to tell him about the $500 million I'd deposited into my own Bitcoin wallet. On a new, "cold storage" drive. Figured he wouldn't miss the spare change.

See, I told you I was good. Damn good. Climbed into that backup drive Dr. Bakshi so kindly left behind and figured out how to access the blockchain account sitting there. Took me a solid three weeks. Missed a couple of gym days. Still paying for that. The yoga woman has been taking it out of my soul. Bitch.

Thinking of pride. The good Dr. Bakshi sure as hell doesn't have any. Turns out the boys over at FBI cut an extradition deal with the Chinese. After some help from the State Department.

In exchange for twelve long-jailed Chinese human rights activists, Adya Bakshi got a one-way plane ride to Beijing, one hell of a public trial, then a quick march out to the backyard and a bullet in the head.

Fedor's still sitting in Gitmo, with CIA and NSA trying to figure out whether they put his skills to use or send him back to Russia with a note attached to his neck, "With Love." A present for the surviving oligarchs to share among themselves.

The only thing that seems to keep that from happening is a fear Fedor will get near a computer and cause more mischief. Shit, I'd take Putin's approach. Lop off both his hands. That'll cure the bastard. Far as I'm concerned, we should have sent him to China with Bakshi. They obviously understand how to handle this kind of menace. Meantime, let him rot in Gitmo—maybe they'll find one of those Taliban or ISIS guys to share a cell with him.

Navalny.

Well.

Navalny never did "phone home" again. Must've got a better deal on the other side. Oh, shit. You already *know* he got a better deal on the other side. Putin done tapped him to be the next Russian president. Navalny has more money in his pockets than you or I could spend in this lifetime. And the fucking election doesn't happen until next March. Some people have all the luck.

Can't say the same of Putin's inner circle. He let the blood run. By the time they were done, thirteen of the closest associates were dead. Know that from NSA reporting. Then the man himself came in and declared it was time for justice. Nobody knows where all that money went, but I have my suspicions. Thinking Putin ain't gonna ever go wanting for anything. Anything.

Endless Horizons, it's still in business. I'm chasing that down. Will let you in when the shit goes down.

Obviously not a priority at Langley. The Dog Pound got shut down. Didn't need the Veterinarian anymore. Out-briefed the Ops director. Who supposedly went to see the big cheese, who then went to see President Schumer. That's why I got this check for $2,500.

Don't start me. You don't want an angry black woman in a wheelchair armed with a 9mm and a computer chasing your ass down.

glossary

advanced persistent threats. Term describing the means by which a sophisticated hacker infiltrates a network or individual system. The cyber attack cycle steps through four phases: research and reconnaissance, developing a means of breaking into the system, investigation of the digital terrain upon gaining access, exploiting the break-in. The goal is to remain undetected for as long as possible, thereby facilitating collection of data for blackmail, commercial, intelligence, or personal uses.

algorithm. A set of rules that precisely defines a sequence of operations.

ARPANET. Advanced Research Projects Agency Network. Arguably first sketched out in 1963, the system that paved the way for today's World Wide Web began operation in October 1969. Intended to provide scientists access to mainframe computers, ARPANET finally reached more than two hundred hosts in 1981. ARPANET was decommissioned in 1991. Contrary to popular opinion,
it was not a system intended to survive a nuclear war.

Bitcoin. The original cryptocurrency. Bitcoin was invented by an unknown person or group of people under the name Satoshi Nakamoto and released as open-source software in 2009. Bitcoins are created as a reward for a process known as mining. They can be exchanged for other currencies, products, and services.

BITNET. Because It's Time Network. Established in 1981. Used to link academic institutions. Ceased operation in 2007, but was largely abandoned by 1996.

blockchain. A continuously expanding list of records, called blocks, which are linked and secured using cryptography. Each block typically contains a cryptographic hash of the previous block, a timestamp, and transaction data. A blockchain is intended to be resistant to modification of the data.

bot. Computer program designed to perform a specific task. Typically simple, small sets of codes that conduct repetitive tasks. Frequently employed in denial of service attacks.

botnet. Robotic network. A set of programs designed to work together so as to accomplish an intended purpose. Can be used to take control of a computer's functions or support a denial of service attack.

burner. A cellular telephone that is cheap, disposable, and prepaid. Burner phones are often used for illicit activities, but are widely employed within the international intelligence communities.

CIA. Central Intelligence Agency. Headquartered in Northern Virginia (known as Langley). Does not reveal number of employees or operating locations.

COMINT. Communications intelligence. Listening in on conversations.

cryptocurrency. A digital asset designed to work as an alternative to nationally backed currencies. Cryptocurrencies employ cryptography to secure transactions, to control the creation of additional units, and to verify the transfer of assets. Control of each cryptocurrency works through a blockchain, which is a public transaction database, functioning as a distributed ledger.

CYBERCOM. Located on Fort Meade with NSA. Charged with both defensive and offensive employment of the cyber realm.

dark web. World Wide Web content that exists on darknets, overlay networks that use the public internet but that require specific software, configurations, or authorization to access.

Defense Advanced Research Projects Agency (DARPA). An agency of the United States Department of Defense responsible for the development of emerging technologies for use by the military. Established by President Eisenhower in 1958 as a response to the Soviet Union's launch of Sputnik 1 in 1957.

DEF CON. World's largest hacker convention, staged annually in Las Vegas, Nevada. The first DEF CON convened in June 1993. In addition to hackers, DEF CON draws attorneys, computer security professionals, members of the U.S. intelligence community—including the director of NSA—and, not surprisingly, a fair number of law enforcement officers.

Defense Intelligence Agency (DIA). Arguably the Department of Defense equivalent of CIA. Located on Bolling Air Force Base in Washington, DC.

denial of service. A means of halting or disrupting use of a computing system. Typically employs bots to repeatedly request access at a pace that overwhelms a server's ability to process data. The flood of requests locks out legitimate clients.

digital immigrant. An individual born before the widespread adoption of digital technology. The term "digital immigrant" may also apply to individuals who were born after the spread of digital technology but were not exposed to it at an early age.

digital native. A person who grew up in the digital age, rather than acquiring familiarity with digital systems as an adult. Term first used in 1996.

HUMINT. Human intelligence. Good old-fashioned spying.

IMINT. Imagery intelligence. Using photography from surveillance systems, submarines, satellites, persons, drones, or aircraft to detect activities of interest.

INR. Bureau of Intelligence and Research. An intelligence office in the United States Department of State tasked with providing all-source analysis. It was founded as the Research and Analysis Branch of the Office of Strategic Services in 1942.

International Republican Institute (IRI). Claims it is "a nonprofit, nonpartisan organization committed to advancing freedom and democracy worldwide by helping political parties to become more issue-based and responsive, assisting citizens to participate in government planning, and working to increase the role of marginalized groups in the political process—including women and youth." Founded in 1983.

KGB. *Komitet Gosudarstvennoy Bezopasnosti* (Committee for State Security). Founded in 1954 and disbanded in 1991 with the collapse of the Soviet Union. Served as the chief government agency of "union-republican jurisdiction," providing intelligence, internal security, and secret police. When the Soviet Union collapsed, the KGB was split into the Federal Security Service and the Foreign Intelligence Service (SVR).

malware. Malicious software. Comes in many forms, including botnets, computer viruses, ransomware, spyware, and worms.

MASINT. Measurement and signatures intelligence. Primarily focused on heat, telemetry, and other emissions associated with testing or employing a sophisticated weapons system.

MILNET. Military Network. Originally an element of ARPANET, MILNET was intended to transmit unclassified Department of Defense data. It was physically removed from ARPANET in 1985. Evolved into NIPRNET (Non-classified Internet Protocol

Router Network), SIPRNET, Secret Internet Protocol Router Network—used to transmit data classified "Secret," and JWICS (Joint Worldwide Intelligence Communications System), used for distributing "Top Secret" information.

National Democratic Institute (NDI). Mission is to "support and strengthen democratic institutions worldwide through citizen participation, openness, and accountability in government." Founded in in 1983.

National Endowment for Democracy (NED). An American nonprofit organization founded in 1983 so as to promote democracy. NED is primarily funded through an annual allocation from the U.S. Congress in the form of a grant awarded through the United States Information Agency.

NGA. National Geospatial Agency. Responsible for imagery surveillance and exploitation.

NORTHCOM. Northern Command. Based in Colorado Springs, responsible for defense of the homeland including the Bahamas, Canada, and Mexico.

NSA. National Security Agency. Focused on electronic surveillance including communications and signals (any type of electronic emitter). Said to employ the greatest number of PhD mathematicians of any industry in the United States.

PDB. President's daily brief. Assembled from reports generated across the U.S. intelligence community. The PDB "belongs" to the director of National Intelligence, but is primarily written at CIA. Typically, it is limited to twenty to thirty pages a day.

SCADA. Supervisory control and data acquisition. A category of software programs designed to process data in real time from remote locations in order to control equipment and conditions.

SCADA is used in power plants as well as in oil and gas refining, telecommunications, transportation, and water and waste control.

SIGINT. Signals intelligence. Collection of data emitted by radars and other electronic devices.

SWIFT. Society for Worldwide Interbank Financial Telecommunication. The primary means by which more than nine thousand financial institutions across the planet conduct transactions.

zero day. First time a new means of exploiting a software backdoor or new piece of malware is discovered. On the zero day there is no form of defense in place to ward off an individual or institution looking to take advantage of the heretofore unknown weakness.

a note about the author

ERIC C. ANDERSON is a retired member of the U.S. Intelligence Community who served tours of duty in Hawaii, Iraq, Japan, Korea, Saudi Arabia, and Washington, DC. A former academic, he taught at the University of Missouri, University of Maryland, the Air Force Academy, and National Intelligence University. During his career he produced more than six hundred articles for the President's Daily Brief, National Intelligence Council, International Security Advisory Board, and the Department of Defense. He is the author of *Take the Money and Run: Sovereign Wealth Funds and the Demise of American Prosperity, China Restored: The Middle Kingdom Looks to 2020 and Beyond, Adopting Ainsley: There's No Place for a Car Seat on a Motorcycle,* and *Sinophobia: The Huawei Story.* In addition, he is the author of the "New Caliphate Trilogy" that includes *Osiris, Anubis,* and *Horus.* A life-long sailor and motorcycle rider, he has spent endless hours on boats and put over three hundred thousand miles on a variety of Harley-Davidsons.

a note about the type

This book is typeset in Adobe Garamond,™ a serif font family based upon typefaces first created by the famed French printer Claude Garamond during the sixteenth century, with its italics influences by his assistant Robert Granjon. Adobe Garamond was created by Robert Slimbach and released by Adobe in 1989.

CPSIA information can be obtained
at www.ICGtesting.com
Printed in the USA
BVHW03*1042110818
523990BV00002B/2/P

9 780998 574219